Billionai Runaway Bride

He's a confirmed bachelor, she's a runaway bride who needs his help.

After confirmed bachelor, Cole Tanner catches the garter at his friend's wedding he finds a dazed and confused runaway bride limping along the back roads of his hometown of True Love, Texas and stops to help.

Tulip Jones obviously can't say no to public marriage proposals—this is her second time to be a runaway bride! She needs help in more ways than one—can Cole teach her how to become a confirmed bachelorette and learn to say no?

They're a perfect match until love gets in the way!

The billionaire bachelors of True Love, Texas are about to meet their matches...

BILLIONAIRE COWBOY'S RUNAWAY BRIDE

Billionaire Cowboys of True Love, Texas, Book One

HOPE MOORE

Billionaire Cowboy's Runaway Bride

Copyright © 2020 Hope Moore

This book is a work of fiction. Names and characters are of the author's imagination or are used fictitiously. Any resemblance to an actual person, living or dead, is entirely coincidental.

CHAPTER ONE

Tulip Jones stumbled out of her car into the torrential downpour. Dazed, she blinked against the rivulets rushing down her face.

Her face hurt.

And her cheek burned.

The world wobbled. She stumbled back on the slick grassy embankment and managed to catch herself before she slipped down the muddy bank. *Where am I?*

The front end of the red car was pushed in against the thick trunk of the tree. It looked as if the car had tried to climb the tree and the headlights beamed slightly upward into the limbs. Rain poured down on her as if God turned a swimming pool over on top of her. Which she probably deserved after what she'd done.

She blinked against the water again and shook her head. She realized the airbag had slammed into her face and probably saved her. She remembered hydroplaning. Remembered hitting the slick spot when the road dipped down, and the feeling of total helplessness as the car lifted on the layer of water and in slow motion turned and then shot off the road, down into the ditch and back up the other side before going airborne and then slamming into the tree.

She'd been driving too fast. In her mind, she'd heard her mama yelling, in her totally Texas twang, Slow down, Tulip Michelle Jones, before you kill us all with your crazy driving.

She ran her hands down her torso, as if making sure her mama hadn't been right and she was actually dead and watching the wreck from up above, before she passed on to the other side.

Nope, she was alive but more than likely only by the grace of God—and an airbag with a great right hook.

She shivered in the rain as fear of what had nearly happened hit her and the knowledge that everything about the last few moments had been out of her control.

Tulip had no idea where she was. Looking down, she realized she was in her wedding dress, and then she remembered…remembered gathering up her long skirt and making a mad run for the church doors. People were watching and she was running…again. Disappointing so many people. If only she'd had the nerve to say no.

No. It was just two little letters and if she'd said the tiny word, everything would have just been so much easier. Tears pricked her eyes, the saltiness mingling with the rain.

She blinked hard into the darkness, the eerie illumination of her car lights the only light anywhere in the wet blackness.

Weak-kneed, she staggered away from the car and stepped into a mud puddle. She pitched forward, then tumbled headfirst to the slick embankment and rolled to the bottom of the watery ditch. Her head hit something hard and the last thing she remembered before she lost consciousness was no one knew where she was and, at this point, probably didn't care. She would probably be headline news tomorrow: Runaway bride dies in ditch after ditching one of Austin's wealthiest bachelors…what a fool. The girl had it made and threw it all away.

* * *

The radio was playing country star Denton McCoy's latest release as Cole Tanner drove through the back-country roads, heading toward his hometown of True Love, Texas.

If it hadn't been for the fact that Cole Tanner knew Denton, he'd have turned the radio off right in the middle of the new hit love song. But he did know Denton, and it felt wrong to turn off his friend's song, so Cole suffered through. But the love song only made his mood all the sourer after what he'd just gone through.

He was heading home now, from attending a college friend's wedding in Waco and had been cornered up by a reporter asking him when he planned to tie the knot with Shelly Duncan the morning talk show host, he'd met at a charity event for saving wild mustangs. He'd realized quickly that Shelly wasn't as nice as she'd first appeared and was only involved in the charity for the good publicity it gave her. He'd also figured out that she'd been dating him for the same reason. He'd broken off their relationship a week before attending the wedding, and evidently news hadn't gotten around. He wasn't one to talk about his personal life.

The reporters just hadn't ever figured that out or cared that he didn't want them meddling in his life. He should have realized his mistake before taking out a local celebrity like Shelly—she wanted all the publicity she could get. They were doomed from the beginning.

Frustrated, he'd left the wedding reception before he could get himself into trouble with the insistent reporter he'd realized was not going to leave him alone. The last thing Cole needed was a tabloid hit piece, and if he didn't get out of there, that's what the reporter would write after Cole told him in no uncertain terms to back off. An article like that wouldn't have helped him or his brothers, but most of all, it would have disrupted his buddy's wedding.

However, on his way out the door, his buddy was tossing the garter, and it flew through the air, over the heads of the pack of single dudes who wanted to catch it, and smacked Cole upside the head. He'd caught it out of reflex.

To catch a garter was the last thing he wanted to do. Especially when he saw lights flash and knew the reporter had caught him in the act.

No telling how that was going to play out on the front page of a tabloid.

He was not ready to get married. That was one thing Cole had put on the back burner. He was busy; he had a ranch to help run and a business that kept him burning the midnight oil. Plus, after Shelly, he was just plain tired of women chasing him for what he could give them. It had been the "curse of the black oil" his little brother Jake always joked about, ever since they'd struck oil in a huge way on their land nearly five years ago. Life had changed for his family overnight, going from a hard-working ranching family to being worth billions. There were great things about it, and not-so-great things.

But he tried to focus on the good that came from it and not the scammers and users who'd crawled out from under their rocks around them at the same time. Not knowing what a person's intentions were when they sought him out was the thing he hated most. He liked nothing about that scenario.

The rain increased, if that were even possible, and he slowed the truck to a crawl as he shoved the thoughts of the garter and reporter to the back of his mind. Rivers in the Texas Hill Country filled fast and flooded quickly here, and he had to give all of his concentration to the road. He tapped a button on the radar on his dash and saw plenty of flash flood warnings. But he knew these roads like the back of his hand, and this shortcut to his hometown of True Love only had one area that would be a major concern; he knew he could turn back if it looked unpassable. His big ole four-wheel-drive Ford truck could handle a good bit of water, so the road wasn't as dangerous to him as it could be for a compact car.

A few minutes later, as he'd maneuvered the crazy zigzagging, rut-riddled blacktop road, he neared the area where it started downhill and flattened out before starting back up. This was the most dangerous area and sure enough, in the beam of his headlights, he could see the water swirling over the road. He also saw a glow up ahead. As he drew closer, his pulse picked up, realizing it was a car. In the darkness, the angle of the lights shining up into the dark trees did not look good. He drove into the water, pushing to drive as fast as he dared in what he thought was about six inches of water and rising fast. If there were someone in that car, he needed to get them out. His lights hit the car. It was a fancy sports car, with its front end smashed into the enormous oak tree. It was crinkled like an accordion, and the driver's side door was open.

Slamming his truck into park, he jumped out. His boots landed in a couple inches of water here—not as deep as the dip in the road, which was good. He jogged through the water and then down into the ditch where the water hit him knee-high. He climbed the embankment and immediately saw that the car was empty. Rain pelted him, coming fast and hard, and he could not imagine that somebody was walking around out here in this.

But somebody had to have been near. The headlights were still on and hadn't clicked off automatically or run the battery down. Standing up, he straightened his cowboy hat, which was doing very little to keep the rain off his face, and scanned the area. The water was rising, so surely whoever it was—if they weren't hurt too bad—had made their way up onto the road. He made his way back through the watery ditch and up the slight embankment. At the rate the rain was coming down, things could get out of control here quickly. It was raining upriver, which would be where the flooding came from when it hit. His worry increased now that he knew somebody was wandering around in this deluge.

Cupping his hands around his mouth like a megaphone, he yelled out. But the way the rain was pounding, he assumed that nobody could hear him holler. Best thing he could do was jump in his truck, drive on down the road and hope he found the car's driver. Unless somebody else had come along right after the accident and picked them up. But this was a very unused portion of road. He put his truck in drive and drove forward, sending up a prayer for safekeeping for the driver. As he rounded a curve in the road, he saw the eerie white form of a woman in a long white dress weaving down the middle of the road. "Thank you, Lord," he breathed out in relief, then squinted through the windshield. What was she wearing? Was that a drenched wedding dress?

The white dress clung to her slender frame and the tail of it dragged behind her in the water. He pulled up behind her, concerned when she didn't seem to hear him. Then she weaved again, and his concern skyrocketed. Something was wrong with her. He pushed the brake, slid the gearshift into the park position, and then jumped from the vehicle into a few inches of water. He jogged through the rain. His boots splashed the water, and he was glad he didn't slip himself because he was wearing his leather-soled dress boots that made dancing at the wedding easier than his work boots, with their thicker sole. Not that he had danced; he had gone to that wedding and gotten out as soon as possible after that reporter had hounded him.

"Ma'am, can I help you?"

She spun and immediately wobbled.

Was she hurt or drunk?

In the beams of his headlights, he could see the cut on her forehead. There was no blood, except a pink film that was there because the rain was pounding down on her. But dazed green eyes sparkled in the lights. She wobbled again and he reached for her arm. "Hold on, I've got you," he said, just as her knees gave way and she started to sink toward the ground. Moving quickly, he wrapped one arm around her waist to hold her up.

She looked up at him. "I think I…need help."

He looked down into her pretty face, and his chest squeezed. She had the sweetest face, even as pale as she was, with those big green eyes.

"Yes, ma'am, you do need help. Come on. I saw your car back there. Now let's get you out of this crazy weather. My truck's just right there and I'll get you to the doctor."

"I don't need the doctor." She shifted away from him.

He held on to her. "Hold on, you might fall."

She looked confused again. "I really don't know what I need. My head hurts." The last couple of words slurred and then she crumbled.

Cole scooped her up into his arms, and she laid her head against his shoulder. A wave of protectiveness hit him like he had never felt in his life before. Holding her close, he stalked through the rain to his truck. Using the hand of the arm her legs were crooked across, he yanked on the handle of the passenger's side and tilted his head at the same time to let the water that had gathered on the brim of his Stetson roll off. This would enable him not to pour it on her as he placed her in the seat. They were both soaked, but there was no reason to add more water to her situation than necessary.

Moving quickly, he got her in the seat and reached across her for the seat belt. While holding her up with one arm; he buckled her in. He yanked on the seat belt so it would lock into place, therefore holding her up because she was passed out—or at least semi-passed out.

As he leaned over her to tighten the strap, she opened her eyes. "Thank you."

The words were a whisper and nailed him to the spot, staring into her emerald eyes. "You're welcome. I'm just thankful—" He didn't finish as her head drooped forward and she was out. Gently, he took her face between his hands and leaned her head back, angled so her forehead rested against the seat belt and the back of her head rested against the far corner of the seatback. She had an angelic face which he knew all too well could be deceptive but still, he wondered, as he closed the door and hurried to the other side of the truck, whether she was as sweet as she looked.

Unfortunately, his personal experience of late told him no. Looks were most often deceiving.

CHAPTER TWO

Not knowing what else to do and very thankful that they had a doctor in the family, Cole headed toward the ranch and called his brother Austin.

"Hello." Austin's groggy voice came over the line.

"Hey, sorry to wake you. I know you had rounds tonight, but I've got a situation. It's flooding out here and on the cut-through to True Love, I found a woman. She'd wrecked her car and was wandering down the middle of the road. She's passed out in my truck right now and I'm heading home."

"Glad you found her," Austin said, fully awake at the realization this was a medical need. He immediately began asking questions about her condition, and Cole filled him in the best that he could.

Finally, he'd answered enough that Austin determined that because Cole was closer to the ranch than the nearest hospital, it would be best to bring her there before going farther in the dangerous road conditions. "Hurry as best that you can—do it safely and I'll be ready."

"Will do." Cole glanced at his passenger. She was still out and that worried him. And he wondered what she had been doing on that road this late at night, alone and wearing a wedding dress.

Was she a runaway bride?

He'd heard of them but so far, never come across one himself. But why else would she be alone and in that dress?

Fifteen minutes later, Cole pulled into the garage where Austin was waiting. His brother had the door opened before Cole could get out of the truck.

Austin looked at him in shock. "She's wearing a wedding dress." He placed his fingers against her pulse.

"Yeah, I didn't take time to mention that part of the puzzle." He climbed out and hurried around to where Austin was finishing taking her pulse.

"Pulse is strong."

Cole let out a breath of relief. "That's good to know. Here, hold the back door and I'll bring her in."

Austin moved out of the way and held the door.

Cole lifted his passenger into his arms, and she roused. "Where am I?"

He held her close, feeling the coldness of her skin and wanting to warm her up. "I brought you to my home to see my brother. He's a doctor, and he's about to check you over."

"Thank you," she said weakly, then rested her head against the crook of his neck.

Austin led the way to the living room, where he'd placed some blankets on the couch to help soak up some of the water as he examined her.

She leaned her head back on the pillow as he moved out of the way and let Austin take over.

His brother sat on the edge of the coffee table and smiled at her. "I'm Austin. Can you look at me and tell me your name?"

She opened her eyes and her brow crinkled. "Tulip Jones."

Cole smiled at her name. It was an unusual but happy name.

"Well, Tulip, as I said, I'm Austin, and this is my brother Cole. He found you wandering on the road. Do you remember that?"

She nodded. Her gaze left Austin and found Cole's eyes and instantly his pulse revved.

Austin patted her arm, bringing her focus back to him. "At least you know who you are. Since we're not sure if you fell and hit your head or what the impact of the wreck did to you, I need to ask you several more questions and do a physical exam of you, your skull and anywhere else you tell me hurts. Is that okay with you?"

"Yes." She nodded. "Just my head hurts and my shoulder and chest."

"Then let's have a look in your eyes first." Austin placed a finger above her eye and tugged upward as he shined a small flashlight into her eyes. "Now, across your ribs where your seat belt probably bruised you."

He pulled out his stethoscope and had her breathe in and out, then gently checked out her collarbone and pressed a few places she indicated were hurting.

"I think you're fine there. Just going to be bruised. Now let me check out your skull."

He watched as Austin gently felt her skull. "Are you starting to feel better?" Cole asked, unable to keep silent any longer.

"Yes. Maybe I was just overwhelmed by all the rain. Everything is a bit fuzzy."

"Do you remember slipping and falling?" Austin asked. "Or hitting your head in the accident?"

Cole watched as his brother placed his fingers into Tulip's thick cinnamon hair and gently felt around. She had beautiful hair. When Austin touched behind her ear she cringed. He lifted her hair out of the way and Cole saw blood.

"Here it is. You have a minor cut and a contusion. I don't believe that is from an airbag. Do you remember falling?" Austin asked.

She looked thoughtful. "I don't remember getting from the car to the road."

Cole wanted to help her, she looked so confused. "Maybe she fell, hit her head and that's why she doesn't remember? She was weaving pretty good and when I reached her, she crumbled."

Austin looked at him. "I'm thinking that's what happened. Tulip, we're going to have to watch you through the rest of the night. And make sure you're not having complications from a concussion. So, we will find you some dry clothes and we're going to let you sleep. One of us will check on you every two hours to make sure you're okay. How's that sound?"

"I hate to impose on you two but I can't go anywhere else, so I'm just going to say thank you. I don't know what would have happened if you hadn't come along, Cole."

"To be frank, I don't either. I'm just glad I took the shortcut through the back roads, or you'd still be out there."

She shivered. "I'm so thankful I'm not."

"Your car is probably totaled."

"It's not mine. It's my fiancé's—I mean, ex-fiancé."

"Speaking of him. Cole said you don't have a phone on you—do you need to use ours to call anyone?"

"No…" her words trailed off, and she leaned her head back as if talking had worn her out.

If Cole's suspicions were right and she was a runaway bride, her fiancé was probably worried about her, wondering where she was, and now he would find out that his car was wrecked, too. Whoever the dude was, he was not having a good day. "Are you sure you don't need to call this fiancé of yours? I can tell you, if I was your fiancé, I'd be worried sick about you."

She didn't open her eyes. "No, I don't feel like it right now."

She was pale and he didn't push. "Is she okay?" He was worried as he looked at his brother.

"She's not with us completely. She'll fade in and out and she can call people tomorrow." Austin stood. "Let's get her to the guest bedroom suite. I have it ready for her."

"I'll carry her." Cole moved to pick her up.

"I can walk…" she said, as weak as a baby kitten's purr.

"I've got you." He scooped her up and held her close as her eyes drifted closed, but not before he saw tears brimming against her cinnamon lashes.

* * *

Tulip woke up in the night in a dimly lit bedroom. She felt disoriented, thirsty, and her head was killing her.

And she was lying in a strange bed.

A table lamp was lit beside a door and softly illuminated the room. She could see that the room beside the lamp was a bathroom. Looking down, she realized she wasn't wearing her wet wedding dress, and vaguely remembered changing clothes. She remembered her rescuer—Cole; she thought his name was. Cole with the golden-brown eyes and the gentle voice.

He'd checked on her a few times, his soft voice rousing her. He was nice. What would she have done if he hadn't shown up when he did? Her stomach growled, reminding her she hadn't eaten since early yesterday morning. And that had only been a half a piece of toast because her stomach had been so upset.

She swung her legs over the side of the bed, and then carefully eased to her feet. The dull ache in her head increased with the movement. She touched the bump behind her ear. The room spun a bit as she took a step forward. The room tilted and she walked uphill, it felt like, and was glad when she made it to the bathroom.

She didn't bother turning on the light, afraid it might hurt her eyes. She left the door cracked and when she was finished, she kept a hand on the wall as she moved around the room to the door that led to the hallway.

She opened the door and poked her head into the hallway. Her stomach growled again, louder. It might have been too nervous to eat before the wedding, unable to keep anything down, but it seemed her appetite was back with a vengeance.

The hall had a lot of doors as she walked along, trailing her hand on the wall for stability. At the end of the hall, she was back in that living room where Cole's brother checked her over.

A lamp illuminated the room, but also a bright moonlit sky shining in from a very high wall of windows she had been too out of it to notice earlier.

She admired the room as she made her way

through it and to the kitchen on the other side. She made it to the island and sank onto one of the plush barstools when the room began to spin around her. The last thing she needed was to fall out on the floor so poor Cole would have to rescue her again. She hated being a terrible ordeal for someone to deal with, and she'd already caused enough problems.

"Hey, are you all right?" Cole came into the kitchen.

She realized in that moment that Cole was one handsome guy. He had longish dark hair, warm amber eyes—full of worry at the moment—and a face that was just very compassionate looking. She enjoyed looking at him. But she liked him for his kindhearted treatment of her. "Hi."

"Hi yourself. You shouldn't be up and about. I came to check on you and got worried when you were gone."

"I'm sorry. I feel bad wandering around your house, but I'm starving. I couldn't eat yesterday because I was so upset and my stomach was churning too badly. Actually, I've been feeling that way ever since my fiancé proposed to me. But it just got terrible yesterday. Terrible enough that I had to admit that I couldn't do it. Anyway, I need something to eat. Do you mind?"

"No, I don't mind. We would have offered but after you got changed into dry clothes, you passed out on the bed."

She tried to remember, but there was still some fuzziness in her brain. "I'm having trouble remembering everything. I don't even remember putting these clothes on."

"Well, I can assure you that you did it on your own. I would have had to get you out of that wet wedding dress somehow, but I was relieved that you had a coherent moment where you could do it for yourself. Although I think you might have my T-shirt on backward. The Texas A&M part goes in the front, not the back." He grinned at her.

She smiled. Her headache was feeling a little better. "I guess I wasn't with it enough to be reading what was on the front of the T-shirt. I'm just glad I have one on."

He stopped with the refrigerator door halfway open and shot her a look over his shoulder. "Yeah, that is a good thing. I would have probably been a shocked to find a strange woman walking around my house half-naked. You would have probably been really embarrassed when you came to your senses."

"You're right. Wow, you barely know me, but you already know me."

He grinned and then looked back at the refrigerator. "Okay, so we've got some cold chicken in here that I can vouch for is the best you'll ever eat." He shot her a nod. "Rose, our cook slash housekeeper, does an amazing job with fried chicken. How does that sound?"

"Wonderful. I love fried chicken. My mama makes some good fried chicken too. Although she hasn't made it in a long time because she's scared of the cholesterol. But I'm not worrying about that right now. Bring it on, Cole."

He laughed and brought the plate over to the island and set it down in front of her. He removed the plastic wrap from the chicken and lay it to the side. The scent was amazing and her stomach growled.

Cole chuckled. "Whoa there, you are hungry. Let me get the lady a plate."

He walked over to the cabinets. Beautiful wooden cabinets, she noticed, with a lovely dark stain almost the color of his rich, dark hair. He opened the cabinet and pulled out two white plates and came back her way. That white plate was just as white as the white T-shirt that he had on with his athletic pants. Her gaze snagged on how the white T-shirt stretched across a very muscular torso.

Trying not to think about his muscles, she reached for the chicken and put a chicken thigh on her plate.

He sat down on the barstool beside her and reached for a crispy thigh too. "I'm sorry—do you want something to drink?" He stood and moved back to the refrigerator.

"I would love some water. That's actually what got me out of the bed first. I was so thirsty."

He pulled out two pitchers. He held them up. "Are you sure you don't want unsweet tea or sweet tea? Rose makes sure we are well stocked on both. Or orange juice? And there are also some sodas in here. Anything you want, I'll make it happen."

He smiled, causing butterflies inside her ribs.

"I'll take water, please. I'm really surprised being a guy that you have unsweet tea in that refrigerator."

"Rose is always trying to get us healthier. She's advocating we drink some unsweet tea during the day instead of the sweet tea. I prefer unsweet tea myself, but I have brothers who live for that stuff, and since they work hard on the ranch, it's not settling around their middles, so they're holding out on Rose's plan."

It wasn't settling on his middle either, she observed. "I'll stick with the water for now, but thanks. I'd opt for the unsweet, too, if I was in the mood for tea."

"Then water it is." He carried two glasses of water over and sat back down beside her.

If she'd been trapped in that car and the flash flood had come along… The thought came out of nowhere and she paused before taking a bite of chicken as reality hit her. She bowed her head and said a prayer of thanksgiving, realizing that if it hadn't been for the Lord sending Cole down that shortcut she might not be here right now. She asked Him if He could have a little more patience with her and help her through the next few days. Because she had a lot of people mad at her right now. She had already been through this once, this runaway bride scenario, and it wasn't as cute as it was in the movies. She hated it. But she kept putting herself in these situations.

She picked up her chicken and took a bite, feeling sullen. She looked up. Cole was watching her.

"You were wearing a wedding dress. Did you run away?" he asked gently.

She nodded and let out a sigh. "I did." She felt terrible remembering the moment when she'd known she just couldn't go through with the wedding.

"What happened? You look like you need to talk about it."

She rubbed her temple, then placed her elbow on the table and plopped her forehead into her palm. "I couldn't say no. If I'd just said no, none of this would have happened." She raised her eyes to his. "It started when he asked me to dinner, and when we arrived, his mother and all of his family were there already waiting on us. I knew I was in trouble when three violinists came out playing and surrounded us. They were playing a very romantic song and my stomach started hurting. Right then and there, I knew I was in trouble, but before I could leave, he went down on one knee and popped the question. Right there in front of his sick mother and the rest of his family. We'd only been dating two months, and I hated to hurt him. He'd already gone through one humiliation, as he called it, when the last woman he'd asked had turned him down in front of everyone."

"Then why did he do it again?"

"I don't know! But if only his sick mother hadn't been there, I might have been able to say no. But she was there, and he'd told me after a few dates that she was dying, and I felt so bad for her. And for him—he was just devastated about it. But he also told me that if anyone said anything to her about her illness that she got very upset, so I wasn't supposed to mention it. To anyone, they were very private about it. Since I wasn't around her often it wasn't that hard not to say anything. But then he brought her to watch him propose to me and I couldn't say no."

"You wanted to say no?"

"That was part of the problem. I tried several times to stop dating him because I was growing uncomfortable around him and knew I needed to be honest and break up. But every time I tried, it seemed his mother would have a turn for the worse, and he was just so upset that I couldn't break up with him when he was so worried and upset. And then he proposed with her there and his extended family. It was an awful situation for me. I couldn't break his heart or his mother's too, so I said yes."

"That doesn't seem fair to you."

She bit her lip and felt terrible. "I thought that way too, but it felt so wrong to hurt him when he was having such a terrible time. And especially since he told me her dying wish was to see us married." Tears welled in her eyes. "So, you see, I broke a dying woman's deathbed wish. I can hardly stand it, thinking about it. If I'd just told him no immediately, it would have been easier on everyone. But I just can't seem to say no to marriage when it might humiliate the guy."

Cole's eyes narrowed. "You say that like this wasn't the first time."

She bit her lip harder and slowly shook her head.

"Seriously, you ran away more than once?"

She nodded. "Twice. See, Joe asked me at a Rangers baseball game. I liked him, but I hadn't fallen in love with him. He loved the Rangers baseball team, and we went to a lot of games. I like baseball, but not that much. One night at a game, the camera put us up on the jumbo screen with a 'Will You Marry Me' written under us. And before I knew what was happening, he dropped to his knee on screen and held out a ring. In front of all those people. I couldn't break his heart." She sighed. "But in the end, I did, and he and his family won't even speak to me. It's terrible. I moved after that and opened my own small business. And then I met Darwin Simpson, and the nightmare happened all over again."

CHAPTER THREE

Cole stared at Tulip. He had never understood the big gesture or whatever women called that where men proposed to them in public places like that on big-screen TVs in front of thousands of people. What did they expect the woman to do when put in that situation? If she had a heart or liked the guy in any way, she would probably say yes rather than embarrass the guy. Him, personally, he thought the dude deserved public humiliation for not thinking about the situation he was putting the woman in. It was different if the two had discussed marriage and he knew she wanted to marry him; then he could understand it better. But both these dudes who'd done this to Tulip did it prematurely, and it sounded as though they'd wanted to trap her. He was not a fan of either man.

Especially this Darwin fella who used his poor sick mother as his ticket to pressure Tulip into marrying him. He chose his words carefully, not saying everything he wanted to say. "For what it's worth, I think neither of them should have put that kind of pressure on you."

She put her chicken down, and a look of conflicted emotions crossed her face. "That's what I think too, but all I can think about with Darwin was his poor mama, and how she must be devastated now at what I did. She just wanted her baby boy to get married while she was still alive, so she could see him happy. According to him, she only has a few months to live."

"That's sad. What's wrong with her?"

"I'm not sure. Darwin talked about her going in for treatments every week and how ill they make her feel. She was a very thin woman and looked weak the times I saw her."

"It's a terrible thing for sure but still unfair to you. You can't marry somebody out of pity."

"I know, but I guess he was desperate."

"Maybe, but that doesn't make it fair to you or right."

She stared at him, as if his words were sinking in. He hoped so, because she was carrying an undeserved weight on her shoulders.

"In my opinion, though it's none of my business, he tricked you." Why was he jumping into her business if it wasn't his business? He didn't jump into people's business normally, but there was just something about the look in her eyes. Of course, it could be the slight concussion that she had, making her eyes look so vulnerable that he had an overwhelming desire to protect her, making his normal thought patterns on not getting involved in people's business fly out the window.

That need to comfort her drove him, and he placed his hand over hers. His pulse beat faster just at the feel of her soft skin. And then her gaze met his, and for a moment, he forgot what he had been about to say. The clock ticked away on the wall. He stared into those deep green pools of her eyes and then, thank goodness, he came to his senses. "You probably need to stop worrying about this right now. You need your rest. Daylight is only about three hours away, and you've been through a lot. Why don't you go back to bed, so you'll be better able to sort through all this?"

She nodded slowly, her gaze continuing to hold his, and he wondered whether the concussion was still affecting her or whether she was just trying to sort through his frank words about her ex-fiancé. Her lips flattened and his gaze snagged on her soft, gently formed lips. Realizing what he was doing, he yanked his gaze back to her eyes, but thoughts of how much he wanted to kiss her remained. What was he thinking?

He pulled his hand away from hers. "Did you get enough to eat?"

"I did, thank you. And you're right, I need to attempt to sleep some more. And you need to, too. Thank you again."

"No need to thank me anymore. Let me help you get back to bed. Things will look better tomorrow. The sun will come up whether or not we want it to, which is always a good thing, and you'll hopefully be thinking better. Austin said that you might have a few blank spots that will fill in eventually. But he'll look at you again in the morning after he gets back from making his rounds at the hospital. And you won't be alone. We'll figure out how to get your car and get you back home."

"I don't know what I would have done if you hadn't found me. You and Austin are wonderful." She stood and then her brows crinkled. "But I just realized that I don't even know where I am. What town am I in?"

He grinned as he carried the plate of chicken they hadn't eaten and placed it back in the refrigerator. "Believe it or not, you're on our ranch just outside True Love, Texas."

"True Love? Oh, I've heard of it. It's very small, isn't it?"

"It's tiny, but its home. Hill Country is riddled with small communities. We only have about a thousand people in the city limits, but the surrounding area's population is big enough to support a diner, a small grocery store, and a few other businesses. Cowboys need to eat and buy groceries."

"It does sound really small. So, what do you do?"

He had taken her elbow and was helping her walk

back down the hall. "I'm a rancher who likes to build things sometimes. Like those cabinets. I enjoy working with my hands, doing woodwork."

"I admired those cabinets the moment I saw them. They're beautiful. You do exceptional work."

"Thank you. I stay busy." He didn't see the need in telling her the cabinets were just a hobby and that ranching was his full-time career.

"It's always nice when people can make a living at doing something they love. I'm blessed that way. Though my business is still new and growing, I'm making it."

"What do you do?"

"I own a little landscaping business. I design beautiful backyards and front yards, and I love it."

"Is your business going to need you tomorrow?"

"No, I cleared my agenda for the next three weeks. Darwin wanted me to take a week off for the honeymoon and then take a couple weeks off to help settle in with his life. He really wants me to give up my landscape business. No, he wanted me to… I'm getting all confused. I keep running what I was supposed to be doing with what I am doing now."

"You're tired." He stopped at her door. "Get some rest. We'll talk about it tomorrow if you want to. It's really none of my business."

"Okay. I think I could sleep for a month."

He watched her go into the room and stood there staring at the door as it closed, then turned and walked slowly down the hall to his room. His mind rolled through all she had said about her fiancé. The jerk had conned her into marrying him because he had proposed to her in front of his sick mama, and then he wanted her to give up her business. Again, it was none of his business, but Cole did not like this guy. Not in the least.

* * *

Tulip had just scooted up to a sitting position a few hours after having eaten chicken in the kitchen with Cole. Their conversation still lingered in her mind as she stared around the room in the daylight. It was a beautiful room, with creamy vanilla painted walls and jade curtains that went well with the comforter's mixture of ivory, tan, and jade tones.

The taupe chair in the corner looked perfect for curling up with a good book. And the soft jade cover thrown across the back kept the theme of the room tied together.

A tap on the door drew her attention.

"Come in." She smoothed her hair and waited, expecting Cole to walk into the room. Her pulse ramped up and then skidded back to normal as Austin entered with a smile on his handsome face. The fact that she was disappointed alarmed her. What kind of person was she to have run away from marrying one man and immediately found herself enjoying the company of another man? But he rescued me. True; that had to be what was going on.

Austin looked weary. "Good morning. You look much better today. How do you feel?"

"Better, thank you. I slept some, though I had an early morning chicken fest in the kitchen with Cole about three a.m."

He smiled. "Cole told me. He said you were moving around better and thinking straighter."

"Yes, then I got tired and I think I started rambling. But my head feels much clearer now."

"That sounds promising. I'm going to look in your eyes." He bent forward. Using his penlight, he checked her eyes and asked a few questions she could answer, thank goodness. "You look good. Are you having any trouble breathing?"

"No. I'm still very sore where the seat belt held onto me, but I'm fine."

"Good to know. Can you stand up on your own?"

She placed her feet on the ground, and then slowly stood up. The room didn't spin or sway. "Nothing is moving." She half laughed with relief.

"That's great. Then I think you're ready. I'd advise you to have your primary physician take a look this week. Cole is taking you home today, so give your doctor a call and set something up soon."

"I will."

He smiled at her. "Perfect."

The skin around his eyes crinkled and again she thought how tired he looked.

"You look weary."

"I am. I had to go check on a patient last night and he had complications, so I haven't slept yet."

"I hope he was okay."

"Sadly, he didn't make it. So, I had to meet with his family. It was heartbreaking."

"I am so sorry."

He looked thoughtful and then nodded. "Me too. Tulip, it was really nice meeting you. I hope you take care of yourself, and I hope one day you find the man who will be right for you and you won't run away from."

"Thank you. I'll never forget you or Cole."

"Nor I you."

Emotion clogged her throat, and she threw her arms around Austin. "Thank you."

He patted her back, and she drew away. He smiled and then walked out the door, but paused to look back at her. "One more thing, Tulip. You're underweight, and I'm assuming since you were in a wedding dress that you must have run away?"

"Yes." It surprised her that Cole hadn't told him.

"That's what I thought. From a doctor's point of view, if you were that upset about getting married that you ran off, and hadn't been eating, then something was wrong. I don't know the facts but just from my limited observation, it sounds like it was probably a good decision. If you ever need anything, you know where to find us. Will you ask us for help if you need it? Cole will give you our information before he leaves you at your home."

How kind was that? "Yes. And thank you," she managed, fighting tears. "Austin, thank you. If I don't see you again, I'll be forever in your debt. And please send me a bill—I'll leave my address for you."

"No charge. I just did what needed to be done for a very nice person. I wish you all the luck in the world."

"You're just as nice as your brother Cole. You're my angels."

"I'm just glad Cole found you, and I was here to help."

She stared at the door after he closed it. Then, with a sigh, she went into the bathroom and stared at herself in the mirror. Oh, my goodness gracious. She looked horrible!

A light but definite blue bruise ran across her eyes

and would probably turn purple soon. She'd known her face hurt a bit from the airbag but when Austin had inspected her face, he hadn't mentioned the bruise, just said everything looked good and nothing was broken.

"Oh, dear." She groaned. It looked as if someone had hit her.

And here she'd thought she was just dealing with a sore knot behind her ear and had just been thankful it wasn't throbbing as bad as it had been.

She couldn't believe Cole or Austin hadn't told her about the bruises. But then, they probably assumed she'd seen them in the mirror and didn't want to make her feel worse about them than she already did. Only, until now, she hadn't felt bad about them because she hadn't looked in the mirror.

Wow, just wow. That airbag had probably saved her life but, boy, it had beat her up in the process. Staring into the mirror she sighed, then realized Cole had been right, her T-shirt was on backwards. She turned it around, then found some new toothbrushes and toothpaste in the top drawer of the bathroom cabinet and took one out. Moments later—feeling refreshed with clean teeth, at least, and wearing her T-shirt correctly—she went to find Cole. And hopefully to eat again. At this rate, the ten pounds she had lost in the course of the engagement were going to come back to her hips with a vengeance, plus more. However, she didn't care; she was so hungry.

And she was looking forward to seeing Cole again.

Maybe, now that she seemed to be thinking clearer, when she saw him, she wouldn't think he was as gorgeous as she had last night. But even if he was, she was going to be immune, the voice in her head declared. Even if he were the best thing since almond chocolate bars, which she loved, she was not interested.

She and dating did not get along.

Until she figured out a way to say no to marriage proposals, no matter how much it hurt the guy, then she would not chance a simple, innocent date with anyone.

She was taking no chances on this happening again.

That meant crushing on her handsome rescuer was out of the question, even if she couldn't imagine Cole doing something so off the wall as to ask her out or ask to marry her. She didn't have any business thinking about him in that way.

Nope, she was most likely doomed to be single for the rest of her life because she was a coward. It hit her as she walked into the kitchen that what she needed was a tutor. Someone to teach her how to just say no, in any situation if she didn't love the guy popping the question. Whether she felt sorry for him or not.

CHAPTER FOUR

Cole did a double take when she walked into the kitchen.

"Yes, my face is blue. And you didn't even tell me."

"I assumed you knew, but last night it wasn't that bruised. Are you hurting?"

"A little throbbing but not bad. I was just startled when I saw myself in the mirror. I know it looks terrible, but I'm grateful I'm alive. I didn't notice earlier because I didn't turn on the main light in the bathroom. The illumination from the lamp in the bedroom wasn't enough to show me the bruises."

"It was only a faint blueish mark last night, and I didn't think it was worth saying anything. You had enough on your mind. Plus, you said your face hurt, and I figured you knew you had some bruising. But it's okay; it will go away. People will understand when you tell them you got hit in the face by an airbag. It's common. I bet you're also sore where the seat belt was."

"Yes, so sore. I guess when I slammed into the tree, it held me in place. Austin said nothing is broken, so that's good."

"Yeah, it is. I have a buddy whose collarbone was broken by a seat belt. Anyway, I bet you're hungry. I have everything set up on the deck outside. I thought you might enjoy some fresh air."

"That sounds perfect. Thank you." She headed to the door as he moved to open it for her.

He was proud of himself; he'd put placemats on the table and set up the silverware. His mother would be proud. He and his brothers couldn't care less about placemats, but he knew his mother was big on setting a nice table for guests, so he'd tried. He was glad he'd done it when Tulip halted and her pretty mouth slack in surprise as she took in the red placemats and the white dishes, the napkin held in the silver napkin rings with a Texas star on them and the silverware. The roses he'd gathered from one of the many rosebushes his mother had planted…and he'd subsequently neglected since she was no longer taking care of them. He had barely given her gardens any thought since he and Austin had been living in the main house.

"How lovely. You didn't have to go to all this trouble."

She stared at him as if he were an alien or something, and that made him chuckle. He felt a bit like one.

"My mom's influence. Plus, after what you've been through, I thought you deserved a pretty table instead of eating cold chicken off a plate straight out of the refrigerator like early this morning."

Her eyes twinkled. "I enjoyed the chicken. But this is above and beyond what you needed to do."

"Please, sit. It's just a table setting. And there is food, too. I promise you it just took a few added steps to getting breakfast done. And to see those eyes of yours twinkle instead of looking dazed and confused is well worth it."

Her hand went to her jaw, and she smiled wider. "Fine. I feel very spoiled at the moment, so mission accomplished." She sat and held her hands in her lap.

"I mentioned to Austin that you looked underweight. No insult intended—I was just worried after you told me you hadn't eaten. He was concerned, too. So I've fixed a lot of bacon and eggs. And these are just some canned cinnamon rolls, but us guys like them, and I thought you might too."

She set her elbow on the table and rested her chin in her palm. "He mentioned it. I told him that ever since the proposal I haven't had much of an appetite and I've lost about ten pounds. But my appetite is back now. He said if I'd been that worried about my wedding, then I probably made the right choice to call it off."

"I totally agree, after what you shared with me. You will have to deal with that at some point, you know."

She sighed. "Please. Not before I have coffee."

He laughed and picked up the silver carafe of coffee and poured her a cup.

"You are a truly amazing man, Cole."

"Some might not agree, but I'm glad I'm impressing you." He grinned and got immense pleasure watching her cup her hands around the warm mug and breathe in deeply.

"Thank you for this." Then she took a dainty sip.

She looked as though her face were hurting. He felt bad for her on that, but her eyes were clearer this morning; they were sparkling green and green apple toned. With her cinnamon-colored hair and her dusting of freckles across her nose, she was beautiful, in a wholesome way.

He sat at the table and lifted the lid of the serving dish. "After you eat, we'll go check on your car and see if it washed away or if it's still there. We'll call the wrecker service once we know what's happened. And also True Love's constable, in case anyone else has spotted the car and called it in. Since it's your ex-fiancé's, you may want to call him and let him know. Or they'll call him."

"Now you're messing with my appetite."

She was still sipping on her coffee, so he placed a

cinnamon roll on her plate, hoping she'd eat the more fattening item. Then added a few pieces of bacon and a large spoonful of scrambled eggs and a spoonful of seasoned diced potatoes. Maybe if he filled her plate up, she'd feel obligated to eat it.

"Just stating facts." He winked at her. "You'll be okay, Tulip."

"I know. And, boy, you are planning on fattening me up in a single meal." She stared at the plate and then laughed. "But it does look delicious."

"And you need it."

She set her coffee down and picked up her fork. "You're right." She cut into the cinnamon roll first and took a bite. She immediately closed her eyes and chewed, a look of bliss on her face.

He swallowed hard, then yanked his gaze off her and took a bite of the sweet roll himself. He loved them and focused on the buttery sweet taste—better to do that than stare at her.

"You're right, that is delicious. Even if it came out of a can. Heated and with that sweet icing, I might eat a second one."

"Have at it. That's what I was hoping."

They both dug in then, eating and talking some. He didn't want to keep her from eating, so he tried not to engage her too much.

After a bit, she set her fork down and picked up her coffee. "I need to take a breather, then that second cinnamon roll is meeting its demise."

He laughed and placed it on her plate as encouragement.

"I guess I can go in your warmup pants and shirt to check on the car. They're swallowing me, but I have the drawstring tightened so they'll stay up and keep me decent. My undergarments are probably soaked, right along with my wedding dress."

He chuckled. This woman cracked him up. "Well, to be honest, I put them in the dryer last night."

"You did?" She blushed. "Awkward but great."

"Yeah, sorry. I assumed you might need them."

"Right. I mean, with this big T-shirt on, I'm not too inappropriate, but I will like having my bra back on. Sorry. We are getting all into my personal business."

He gave a crooked smile. "You're not inappropriate. I just thought you might want them, so I picked them up. But getting back on track, my brother Levi is picking you up some clothes at Walmart. He volunteered to make a run there for you when he found out what had happened."

"That is so nice—"

As if on cue, Levi walked out onto the patio. "Did I hear my name?" He was carrying a plastic bag. Levi also had a newspaper—or what Cole had a sneaking suspicion was one of those gossip tabloids from the checkout line at the store. He cringed at the sight.

"Hey, Levi, right on time. Tulip Jones, this is my younger brother Levi."

"Hi, Tulip, very nice to meet you." Levi tipped his hat and gave that half grin of his that had most females around chasing him.

"It's so great to meet you, Levi." Tulip looked up at his brother with her big green eyes and it was Levi who looked startled, and stuck staring.

"Um, you, too. I'm sorry about the accident. It's a shame to have that bruise on that pretty face of yours. I hope it doesn't hurt too much."

She shook her head. "Not bad. I'm sure if I smacked my face on something, it would hurt worse, but right now it is manageable."

Levi laughed. "Well, that is good to know."

Feeling a prick of jealousy that he shouldn't be feeling, Cole cleared his throat. "Levi, did you get the clothes?"

Levi tore his gaze off Tulip and looked at Cole. His brother's expression told him Levi knew Cole wasn't happy with him ogling their guest.

"I sure did." He looked back at Tulip. "I'm glad my brother came along and rescued you last night. We would not have wanted to have some grim news in the paper this morning."

"I am, too, and I keep telling him he's my angel, and Austin as well. And now you for bringing me these clothes. I'm so happy to have them."

Levi grinned, and a dimple showed in his left cheek as his eyes danced. "I'm happy to make you happy. Now, as for you, big brother, I hate to break it to you, but you have made the headlines once again." He pulled the folded paper from under his arm and slapped what Cole could clearly see was a tabloid onto the table.

Cole's stomach soured. Practically covering the front page was a picture of Cole getting hit in the face with that bride's red garter. And someone had photoshopped into the picture a very shocked-looking Shelly Duncan. The headlines were lousy: Local billionaire cowboy and fiancée, television personality Shelly Duncan, having a fight at a wedding venue last night over their own upcoming wedding.

Cole had to hold back his temper as a sudden gasp rang out from Tulip. "That's where I know you from! You're Cole Tanner, the billionaire cowboy who dates Shelly Duncan, the Good Morning Hill Country host." Her eyes were wide, as if suddenly seeing him differently.

He hadn't mentioned his last name because of this very reason. He'd wanted her to look at him as just some good ole boy from True Love, Texas, for a little while. But her reaction didn't settle well on his already sour stomach.

"Yup, that'd be me," he said, stiffly.

Levi laughed. "That's my big brother, dating a local celebrity. Which I've already warned him was not a good idea. We already don't like having the paparazzi chase us around, and then he goes and dates her anyway and then breaks up with her and he gets this…his face plastered across every gossip rag in the checkout line."

"Levi," he warned, trying to keep his temper in check.

His brother didn't heed his warning. "I can't stand the vultures. I'm sure if they ever hounded you, Tulip, you'd agree with me. They're worse than fleas. They get under my skin and make me itch."

Tulip's mouth moved, but nothing came out as she stared at Cole. She tried again. "I can't form any words. I thought you were just a cowboy."

He held her gaze. "And that's not the reaction I like to get from people when they find out who I am. I'm still the same guy who rescued you last night. Just a cowboy who came along and did a good deed."

She looked horrified. "I'm sorry, I was just surprised. I didn't mean to react so shocked."

Cole tried to not let her reaction to finding out who he was disappoint him, but it was exactly the reaction he couldn't stand. And here he had thought maybe, just maybe, she would be different.

"Yeah, well, that's what happens when you date a celebrity, all right. Anyway, enough about me. I told Levi about what size I thought you might be, told him to get you some things in size small. Hopefully, you'll find some things in that bag that fit. I've got to go make some phone calls and then I'll come back after you finish eating and change clothes. We'll go look for your car. Then I'll take you home."

With that, he stood up, turned and walked out of the room. He could feel Tulip's gaze on him as he went. Everything in him told him to turn around and go back, but he needed the distance between them. He needed to get his head on straight.

If there was one thing he hated more than fake tabloid stories, it was people who treated him differently when they learned who he was.

CHAPTER FIVE

Tulip watched Cole walk into the house, confused by what had just happened. She shot her gaze back to Levi. He looked from the door back to her and looked about as enthralled, as if he were watching a favorite TV drama.

"Did I just make him mad?" The very thought made her feel sick.

Levi let out a lengthy breath and reached for a piece of bacon. "That would be a yes. You just pushed his trigger points. If there's one thing my brother can't stand, it's somebody thinking different or treating him different after learning who he is. You know, about all that money. He can't stand it."

"But, I was shocked because I finally connected

him with dating the host of that morning TV show. I usually watch it every morning. It had nothing to do with money."

Well, maybe. These guys were billionaires, and it was a bit of a shock knowing how down-to-earth they'd been, and she never suspected who they were. Not even from the looks of the ranch. It looked like a regular ranch—not extravagant—full of hard-working cowboys and herds of cattle.

"He's a good guy," Levi assured her. "I'm sure when you explain that all to him, he'll be fine. So just tell him."

"I hope so. He's been nothing but nice to me. But, to be honest, it's not like I meet a billionaire every day. Now, Darwin, my ex-fiancé—he had money. Not nearly a billion, but he liked for people to know. I'm not the kind of person who treats people differently when I learn that they have money or no money. I don't really care; I just was shocked that he was the guy who dated Shelly. I had seen him in the paper. I'm really digging a hole for myself, aren't I?"

Levi laughed, and his eyes twinkled. "You're fine.

But let me give you a word of advice. My brother tends to be a bit serious, however he doesn't hold grudges, so you'll be all right. From what he told me, you're a good person. This Shelly thing just has him in an uproar. They're done, and she's not liking it. I don't care what that tabloid says—nothing is true. Take it from me, we've been overnight billionaires for the past five years, and in that time we've all had our share of distorted, untrue cover stories written about us. They take a picture and photoshop it how they want and then write whatever they want to create the drama they want. Shelly wasn't even at that wedding he was at last night, and that article makes it sound like she was and they had a blowup."

"Really?"

"Read it. It's entertaining but totally untrue. The only real thing that did happen was that garter hit him in the face as he was leaving to avoid the press. They made up a story anyway."

"That is just wrong. I bet that was a shock to become overnight billionaires."

"Oh, it was for certain. We're still not your normal

billionaires. We ranch just the way we always did, just a bit bigger and bolder. And have a few more headaches—like tabloid stories and women chasing us all the time." He winked at her.

She laughed. Levi was funny. She had a feeling he wasn't really joking about the women chasing him. "I bet you can handle that just fine."

"I do pretty well with it. But Cole, he's become pretty wary of dating, and this fiasco with Shelly is only going to make him worse."

She hated that he'd gone through that. "I don't read those magazines, so I wouldn't have known who any of you were, except that I recognized him because he dated Shelly. Even if a person doesn't read them, his picture's been on the magazine facing the checkout line. Plus, my mama is a beautician and runs a small beauty parlor next to her house. There are stacks of those magazines in there. I might have seen it on one of those when I dropped by to visit her at some point."

"And Cole will realize he's being too touchy on this subject. It's just we are all at the stage of growling when it comes to paparazzi or reporters hounding us for the money they can make off a made-up story."

"I can understand that."

"Anyway, if you're finished eating, you should go change into your new clothes. I tried to pick some pretty colors." He grinned. "I hope they fit. I got two different sizes of everything, just in case. Um, ahh, even some um…underwear. I just grabbed one of those bags with six pairs in it." He looked as uncomfortable as he sounded, then rushed on. "Anyway, when you're ready, find Cole and while y'all are out and about looking for your car, explain things to him again. It'll all be fine. One thing about Cole is he's fairly easy going. He'll probably apologize to you. And if he doesn't, I'll take him out behind the barn and set him straight." He winked again, grabbed a cinnamon roll and headed off the end of the deck.

"Thank you," she called.

He grinned over his shoulder. "I hope everything works out for you. I've got some cows I've got to go brand. My cowboy crew is waiting on me, but it was nice meeting you, Tulip." He tipped his hat and strode down the sidewalk and toward the barn across the rock drive.

She watched him go and felt a little better after talking to him. Picking up the bag of clothes, she headed inside. It was time for a shower and fresh clothes. All a wonderful thing before she faced the day. Meaning, facing Darwin. It had to be done.

But it was Cole she was most worried about facing.

* * *

Cole found Tulip standing in the front yard, studying the big stone ranch house. Quintessential Hill Country with its white stone and cedar post and beams with sidewalks and patios all around made from sandstone. The place had been his mother's pride and joy. Still was; she just wasn't here to keep it up and enjoy it since she was happily enjoying traveling the world and living in Florida when not traveling.

"My mother planted all of this and designed the patios that are scattered around. She's enjoying the life of retirement now and traveling with my dad, so it was left to me to oversee the upkeep. As you can see, I've done a poor job. I have the yard guy come in and keep it looking decent but it looks a bit tired, don't you think?"

"It needs a little tender loving care is all." She shaded her eyes to look at him.

He realized she didn't have sunshades. Or he regretted the idea that she might be shading her eyes from him because he'd stalked out on her earlier like a baby. Guilt raked through him like hot coals being scraped across his conscience. He hadn't expected her reaction at finding out who he was, and he hadn't figured out why her reaction had disappointed him so much. But get over it, already—her sudden and wide-eyed reaction had been what it was. She'd said she watched Shelly's morning show and so, of course, if she saw a tabloid with her picture on it sitting on the magazine rack beside a herd of different flavored gum and candy bars in the checkout line, it would be normal for Tulip to read the headlines. That didn't mean she'd bought the trash magazine or believed what it said.

The truth was, he had been dating Shelly and that wasn't reported wrong. He didn't know what else was in the magazine, but until he read it, he couldn't say it was all lies. He'd have to make himself read it later. But for now, he had more important things to take care of.

He pulled his Stetson from his head and held it between both hands as he held Tulip's gaze. "Tulip, I need to apologize to you. I'm sorry about earlier. I overreacted and acted like a petulant child. You didn't deserve that behavior from me, and I'm embarrassed I did that. Please forgive me."

She lowered her hands and stared at him, her pretty eyes crinkling at the edges as they fought off the bright sunshine. "You don't need to apologize, Cole. Really, I just reacted out of shock because I remembered seeing your face when in line at the grocery store. Plus, like I told Levi, my mama has a little beauty shop next to her house, and she and her ladies love those magazines. They might not believe everything in them, but—I hate to tell you this—they sure think the stories are entertaining." She sighed. "I might have seen you on one of those covers when I went to her shop. Plus, like most of Texas, I heard what happened with you and your family striking such a vast oil reserve on your family land. There is just no getting around it—the bump on my head had me not putting two and two together until Levi plopped that magazine down in front of us."

He sighed this time. Everything she said was the truth. "All pointing to the fact that I reacted badly. So, can we drop all that and start back where we were before the boy child came out in me?"

She laughed. "We could but the elephant's in the room—there is no hiding the fact that you do have all that money and I know it. But I can assure you that I am not coming after you for your money. I will not give you any special treatment or favors because of your money, so, cowboy, don't expect anything. And I cannot loan you any money since I'm pretty sure my bank account is much smaller than yours. So, can we agree on that being the way things are?" Her lip twitched and her eyes sparkled in the sunlight.

He relaxed and smiled. He liked this woman. "We can agree."

"Great. Now, just for the record, I bet it does

irritate you when you get your picture put on the front of those tabloids. I would hate that so much. That's why you can rest assured I am not going to be coming after you for a date or a marriage proposal, because no amount of money could entice me to give up my privacy. I feel awful for you. I read that article and whew…whoever marries you will have to be okay with all of that because the tabloids love you and the girlfriend or wife will find herself on the cover. You have stirred the pot with dating Shelly Duncan. Do you know that the article says that you and Shelly are having a baby together?"

His insides turned icy cold. "Are you serious? Believe me, I can assure you that that is not true."

"Whether it's true or not, that's what it says."

"Perfect. Just perfect. This is ridiculous. Come on, Tulip, we need to get you to your car."

They headed into the garage. He opened the truck door for Tulip and wondered what she was thinking of him.

She placed her hand on his arm before he closed the door. "I'm sorry you're having to deal with this."

"Me too. I'm still processing it. Trying to understand why she would lie about something like this. But also, who is to say she really said it."

"True. Maybe she didn't actually."

He closed the door and then headed to his side of the truck.

Maybe it was all fake. Surely Shelly had not gone and gotten pregnant somewhere. Those tabloids—man, they were just liars. Whatever sold a story, they used it. Clickbait was the name of the game: whatever headline could get people to click and make the magazines money. He was walking, talking clickbait. He got a headache just thinking about it.

He had to figure out what in the world he needed to do to make sure that nothing in that article would come back and bite him in the rear. That was a certainty. He needed to call his lawyer and put Harold on it. This was one story he wasn't just going to take sitting down. He had not fathered a child with Shelly, and he would not let this go.

CHAPTER SIX

When they neared the area where the car was, the creek had risen and the road was impassible. At least four feet of water prevented cars from crossing the dip in the road. But Darwin's car was exactly where it had been when Cole had last seen it. Water was up to its doors because it was on an incline which had saved it from at least washing downstream.

"Well, there she sits. She didn't get swept away. So that's a good thing. I think we better call the constable and a wrecker and let them know it's here." He studied the car, his mind clicking on a factor he hadn't thought of yet.

"If you ran out of the church, how did you get the key to the car?"

She bit her lip and cringed cutely. "It was kind of a premeditated situation. I was thinking about it almost from the beginning but talking myself out of calling off the wedding. And, well, actually the dress I picked had a deep pocket hidden in the folds and that swayed my liking the dress. I slipped the key in the pocket and had it with me when I walked up the asile."

He threw his head back and laughed hard. A premeditated runaway bride situation from this soft, gentle looking woman was just funny to him. This Darwin jerk just thought he'd found a little mouse he could bully. She'd totally surprised him Cole figured when she ran away.

"You are full of surprises, Tulip."

She blushed and he couldn't take his eyes off of her. The sound of sirens had them both turning toward the road.

"Speaking of the constable, there he comes. Brace yourself."

They watched the big white boat of a car the constable of True Love drove. It was approaching at a fast pace, with lights flashing and siren blaring. Of course they were. Cole dreaded any time spent around Virgil Redding. They did not get along. The man was old enough to be his granddaddy's granddaddy—not really, but he looked it—and he was about as grouchy as they came.

They watched the vehicle skid to a stop. Virgil got out of his car, a skinny-as-a-stick fella. He yanked his khaki pants up to his navel, then strode their way.

"Hey, Virgil, you come to check out this vehicle?"

"Somebody called it in, and they said it was bad. I needed to come see if anybody had been hurt. What are you doing here, Cole Tanner?"

"This is Tulip Jones. When I was passing through here last night before the flood happened, I came upon this wreck. It was late, about eleven o'clock. And I found Tulip here wandering down the side of the road. She'd hit her head on a rock after she fell, we think. Austin checked her out, and we kept her at the house and checked her all night for a concussion. She's better this morning, so we came to check on the car. We were just about to call you and let you know about it, and call a wrecker too."

"Why didn't you call me last night?"

"Because I didn't see a need in it, and it was pouring down rain. You didn't have any business down here either. I thought it would be floating downriver this morning."

"You don't need to tell me what's my business and what's not my business, Cole Tanner."

"Virgil, can we just move past this? Like I said, you and my granddaddy had y'alls little feud and I wasn't a part of that. If you could just forget about it and take care of this car, I'm going to take Tulip to her house after we get the car situation figured out."

Virgil frowned at him and then, looking as if somebody had squeezed his belt too tight, he stormed over to where he could see the license plate on the car. He made a point of jotting it down on his little white piece of paper in the little white notepad that he pulled out of his pocket, and then he stalked back to his car.

"He acts like he got up on the wrong side of the bed this morning."

"Every morning, you mean. That man is in a sour mood all the time. He's never been the same, they say, after my granddaddy stole the woman he loved. He held a grudge for my granddaddy and hasn't gotten over it all these years. And he's not my fan these days."

"And why is that?"

"Because he's got a granddaughter who had a crush on me, and I didn't reciprocate. And you'll learn one thing about me—I don't date people just on a whim or because I feel sorry for them. Or because they just happened to be around when I feel like dating someone. When I date somebody, there's something about them that I really like, and I think that maybe there's a possibility that somewhere down the road she'd make a good wife. I hate to admit it, but I've been a poor judge of character a few times. Shelly Duncan tops that list."

She stared at him, and then he frowned.

"Okay, strike that." He rubbed his neck and felt terrible. "Shelly and I didn't get along and she wasn't the person I thought she was, but that didn't give me any right to say that. So just forget I said that."

She laid a hand on his arm. "It's totally

understandable. Sometimes you just have a bad day and you've had a lot thrown at you this morning, so relax—I'm not holding anything against you."

Staring into Tulip's eyes, Cole couldn't look away.

* * *

Tulip liked this guy even more as she watched him struggling with having said something that wasn't exactly nice about the woman he'd dated. Even if she suspected it was probably truthful.

Truthful. She hadn't been truthful her entire time of being engaged to Darwin. If she had been, she would never have said yes to his proposal. That bothered her. As she stared at the car crinkled against the tree and so close to the water that could have swept her away, she knew she could have been dead this morning. And all because she couldn't say no when she most needed to.

She had been given a second chance, and looking at that red, crinkled-up front end of that Corvette, she knew it could have been so much worse in so many ways.

"Virgil, why are you looking like that?" Cole asked.

Tulip turned away from staring at the car to see what Cole was talking about. The constable was coming back from his car, and he was staring at her with beady little eyes and a grim set mouth. She got a really bad feeling suddenly that something was really wrong.

And then he pulled out his handcuffs and drew his gun.

"What?" she gasped.

His gun shook slightly as he pointed it at her. "Tulip Michelle Jones, you are under arrest. You have the right to remain silent. Anything you say can and will be used—"

"Now hold on, Virgil. What are you doing?" Cole bellowed harshly. His amber eyes practically flashed gold flames as she stared at him in bewilderment. He was furious as he stepped in front of the cop with the slightly shaky gun. "Put that dang gun away before you shoot someone."

Tulip pushed on Cole. "Move—he might shoot you, and I couldn't live with that. What did I do? Why are you doing this?" She pushed on Cole again, but he was rock solid and didn't budge.

"You are a car thief. You stole that car and you are a wanted woman."

"I'm warning you to back off, Virg—"

"Cole, I didn't steal the car. It belongs to Darwin, but—"

The old man stepped closer. "It's been reported as stolen and also that you may be armed and dangerous. Now move out of my way, Cole Tanner."

She gasped. "Dangerous?" Fury heated her skin to a glowing point, she was sure. "I'm going to kill that man."

"Are you making threats? I'll have to add that to your long list of infractions."

Her eyes flew wide open. "I didn't mean that. I was his fiancée. I drove that stinking car to the church for the wedding because he insisted. He wanted me to arrive in style. I did not steal it. How was I supposed to run away from the wedding when I didn't have my own car there to leave in?"

"Lady, I don't have any idea what you're talking about, but the facts are you stole somebody else's car and I am here to arrest you. Now let me put these handcuffs on you. I'm taking you in."

"You are doing no such thing. Put that gun away." Cole tensed; she hung onto his arm with a death grip and his bicep tightened up.

"I am taking her to jail, and you are obstructing the law. If you don't step out of the way, I will take you in, too, Cole Tanner. And I will enjoy it," he snapped.

She did not like this little mean man and realized that if she didn't do something fast, Cole was probably going to go to jail too. This was her humiliation and he didn't deserve any more trouble because of her. After everything he had done for her, she just couldn't bear it if this bitter man got the chance to take Cole to jail. Especially considering it was very obvious Virgil would love nothing more than to do exactly that.

She stepped out from behind Cole. "I'll go with you. Cole, you do not need to get involved in this. Just calm down."

He stepped in front of her again. "No. I'm not letting him take you in."

She looked at him, feeling a little lost and completely confused, like she had been since she had left the church. "Cole, he's the law, and he's right. I do have to go with him. And if you obstruct my arrest, then you would have to go too. Please, just stay here. And I hate to ask you, but I might need a lawyer if you know one." She'd never needed a lawyer and had no idea who to call, so she hoped he might know someone.

He pulled his angry glare from the constable to stare at her.

"Please, don't get thrown in jail because of me, Cole," she implored of him.

His eyes softened. "All right, I will let you go with him. And believe me, I know some lawyers, my lawyers, and I am calling them the moment Virgil drives away with you. But don't worry, I'll be right behind you and watching every move he makes."

"Thank you. And I am so sorry that I drug you into this. I don't know what Darwin's doing."

She turned so her back was to Virgil, and she put her hands together behind her. She jumped as the cold metal of the handcuffs touched her skin. It was humiliating. And then the feel of them fastening had her fighting back tears. She kept them at bay, though, because she didn't want Cole to see. Her whole world seemed to be crashing down around her, even imagining that she would go for the rest of her life with a criminal record.

Would he take her to the jail, take her photo and book her?

Suddenly she thought of all those terrible pictures of people who were being booked at the jailhouse and how horrible they looked in their pictures. Pictures splashed all over Facebook and the newspaper. It was mortifying. The tears pricked and the edges of her eyes dampened despite fighting them off. Her gaze went to Cole, seeking his steady, strong presence to calm her.

But the moment she saw the stricken expression on his face, she had to blink back the tears more. But she was alive, the voice in her head yelled as it was being drowned out by all the negative emotions. And

Cole Tanner was going to help her. She hated dragging him into this, but right now he was her only hope… And Darwin? Well, she might be a pushover, but as of right now, if he came within ten feet of her, he'd better run.

* * *

Cole had to fight hard not to push Virgil away from Tulip. Watching her be handcuffed because this Darwin wimp had set the cops on her out of spite had him seething. He knew there were two sides to every story but in his heart of hearts; he didn't believe Tulip was lying.

Until he knew different, he refused to even consider it. He didn't look too deeply at why he was so set on her being exactly who she portrayed herself as being. He wanted her to be as sweet and good as she seemed to be. He'd known her less than twenty-four hours and something about her got to him. Pulled and tugged and had him roped in with every smile and soft look of her eyes.

Watching her be put in the back end of that stinking constable car infuriated Cole. He had never been as mad in his entire life. He had just thought he had been angry a time or two, but never anything like this. Cole had already not liked Darwin because of the way it seemed he conned Tulip into accepting his marriage proposal. When she'd told him how he'd conned her into marrying him by using his mother's illness as an excuse, Cole had believed he was a manipulative jerk. Cole wondered whether Darwin's mother was even sick, as Darwin had claimed. Why else would he make it so important that Tulip not mention anything about the illness when around his mother?

Something about the whole thing stunk, and he planned to find out everything. He got in his truck. There was one good thing about striking all that oil and becoming a billionaire like they were, he and his family—they had a whole legal team behind them. A team that was the best at what they did. Darwin would not want to tangle with them.

Especially when they would be acting in the interest of a sweet lady like Tulip.

He had never been so thankful for anything in his entire life. And it was a first; for the longest time, he had almost looked at that money as a curse, just like his brother Levi had said. But today it was a blessing, and he planned to not waste it.

He moved toward the car. "Tulip, you hang in there. I'll be right behind you and I'll be making phone calls, so don't you worry." He took a step toward Virgil as the cop closed the door on Tulip. "And, Virgil, I'm warning you, you better not book her. And I'd better not see a picture of her put all over the place or I'll have your hide."

"Are you threatening me?"

"Let's just say I'm just looking into your future. No, I'm not threatening you…I'm just stating a fact."

Virgil got in his car and slammed his door.

Tulip's window was rolled up; she couldn't hear Cole, so he placed his hand on the window. Tulip couldn't place her hand on his because it was handcuffed behind her back. Her big eyes implored him from behind the glass and his heart broke. Then, she leaned her forehead against his palm, with the cold, hard glass between them.

Virgil pressed the gas and Cole stepped back and watched as he shot forward with so much force Tulip's head jerked back as the car lurched forward and flew over the hill, sirens blaring and lights flashing.

"That is just pathetic. Barney Fife, I'm coming for you," Cole muttered. He got in his truck and then he pressed the speaker button on his steering wheel and he started making phone calls.

* * *

Tulip wanted to throw up her breakfast as Virgil pulled up to the sheriff's office.

This was really happening.

He got out of the car and pulled open her door. "Okay, out of the car," he said.

The only good thing was he didn't pull his gun on her.

She stared at the sheriff's office and she felt like a thousand-pound weight sat on her shoulders, knowing she had to walk inside the building. She placed her feet on the ground and then scooted to the edge of the seat and stood up, not as easy as usual with her hands handcuffed behind her back.

"Go on, walk. This will teach you not to steal cars."

Ignoring the awful little man, she started forward. Panic clawed its way up her throat with each step she took. She wanted to turn and run the other way but that would be a terrible mistake, so she focused on the one positive she had in all of this terrible situation: Cole was on her side. That knowledge calmed her some because she trusted him as he was holding her future in his hands.

Sucking in her breath to push back the panic, she stepped forward and walked toward the doors.

CHAPTER SEVEN

Cole followed the cop car. "Harold, she didn't steal the car." Harold owned the law firm that represented Cole and his family. "I want you here as quick as possible, before they decide to book her." He filled Harold in on everything that had happened.

"I'm on my way. It'll take about forty-five minutes, but I'll get her out when I get there. So the ex-fiancé is holding a grudge, you think?"

"It's the only thing I can come up with. He's getting back at her is my suspicion."

"Nice guy." Harold's words dripped with sarcasm

"Tell me about it. And that's after he guilted her into accepting his marriage proposal in the first place." Cole explained that statement as he slowed, entering town. "And not only did he accuse her of stealing his car, he told them she was armed and dangerous." That infuriated Cole.

"He's a real sleazeball. I'll be there shortly. And everything is going to be fine."

"I'll meet you there." As soon as Cole ended the call with Harold, he speed-dialed his investigative contact.

Jensen picked up on the first ring. "Morning. You're out and about early."

"It's not that early and I've got a job for you," Cole cut to the point.

"Well, this sounds serious, Cole. I don't believe I've ever heard you this angry."

"I've never been in a situation like this. I need you to dig up everything you can on Darwin Simpson and I need it as fast as possible. I want the preliminary in like the next hour, and then you keep digging and you dig as deep as you need to go because this little dude is about to find out he messed with the wrong person."

"I'll have it for you. I have a feeling that whatever he did to you, he will regret it."

"Not to me, but to a very nice lady."

"Even more regret about to happen."

"Depends on what you dig up. I have a hunch it won't take long to find something. He's playing dirty and I'm not a fan." Cole hung up, telling himself he needed to calm down, but he wasn't going to. He reached the sheriff's office and walked inside, scowling.

The older lady behind the counter looked up from behind her skinny glasses. "Can I help you?"

"I hope so, ma'am. I'd like to see Tulip Jones. The constable just brought her in."

"Can I have your name?"

"Cole Tanner. I've got a lawyer on the way for Miss Jones, and I want to make sure everyone back there understands that nobody better interrogate her or ask her any kind of questions without her lawyer present."

"Let me go get the sheriff."

"That would be good." He watched her hurry through a door next to her desk.

Moments later, the sheriff walked out to meet him.

"I'm Sheriff Jordan Billings. I hear you're asking some questions. Can I help you?"

"I'm Cole Tanner. The constable out of True Love, Texas, just brought in Tulip Jones. I'm here to act as her advocate until her lawyer arrives. He is on the way and she is not to be asked any questions until he gets here."

"We have her in a cell and we'll wait for her lawyer."

"Can I see her?"

"Sorry, but no."

He stared at the man, who was about his age. From everything he knew about the man, he was supposed to be a fair man. "In that case, I'll wait outside, as long as I have your word that she's being treated fairly."

The sheriff nodded. "It's the only way I do business. You have my word."

"Glad to hear it. But tell Virgil that."

The man's jaw ticked. "I'll do that. Retirement is almost here and then his jurisdiction can stop voting him into his position."

"I feel better knowing we agree on that issue." He didn't go into any more depth. Rumor had it that Virgil was finally giving up his position making way for a younger retiree to get elected. The tiny jurisdiction of True Love didn't have a big budget, considering if you blinked twice, you'd miss the caution light driving through town, not even realizing you'd passed through the town.

He decided to wait outside for Harold. The helicopter would land in a field barely three blocks away and from where Cole was leaning against the tailgate of his truck. He was restless, thinking about Tulip sitting in a jail cell. He was trying to distract himself by watching cars and trucks drive by, and people coming in and out of the Bluebonnet Diner, which was across the street. He wished the helicopter Harold was riding in would fly faster. He checked his watch. He had about forty minutes to wait…

* * *

Thirty minutes later, Cole was reading a text from

Harold stating that he was ten minutes from landing when a news van pulled into the parking space in front of the sheriff's office. Cole groaned. Just to be safe, he pulled his Stetson low over his eyes.

A sleek, black BMW pulled in beside the van and a small guy dressed in a pink shirt, white golf shorts, and loafers with no socks climbed out of the BMW. Cole had a bad feeling he knew exactly who he was looking at. And he didn't like him being here one bit.

The guy wore a smug look on his face as he spoke to the female reporter who was holding a microphone. A guy in a grey suit got out of the passenger's side of the car and the entire group headed toward the sheriff's office.

Cole sent Harold a text that the ex had arrived with an entourage, and he was going inside to see what was going on. He slipped into the lobby unnoticed and moved to the side, where he could lean against the wall and listen.

"I'm Darwin Simpson and I believe you've arrested my ex-fiancée who stole my car and my pistol?"

The woman looked nervous as she saw the cameraman pointing the big video camera straight at her. She stood, gave a nervous smile, and hurried back through the door she'd disappeared behind earlier. He suspected the sheriff would show up soon.

Cole wasn't liking the fact that good ole Darwin was about to attempt to humiliate Tulip. It was the only explanation he had about the cameras being here.

Almost instantly, the sheriff came into the room. He calmly looked around the lobby. His gaze rested on Cole before settling on Darwin. He completely ignored the cameras. "Can I help you with something?"

"I understand you have arrested my car-thieving ex-fiancée? She ran out on our wedding last night and stole my car and my gun. I'm here to press charges."

"Well now, I hate to disappoint you, but we've just brought her in for questioning. We're waiting for her lawyer to arrive before we proceed. We understand there are some extenuating circumstances about the car."

Darwin's face reddened. "There are no extenuating circumstances. That's exactly what she did. And I demand you book her."

The sheriff's expression barely changed, but Cole saw the tightening around the edges of his eyes. "Last time I checked, they elected me sheriff around here and I run the show in this town. So, I suggest that you and your circus here get out of my lobby and let me do my business."

"I don't like being treated like this. And my lawyer will take it up with you," Darwin warned.

"That's fine, but those cameras need to be outside."

"I want them here."

Darwin and the sheriff were exchanging more words when Harold walked into the lobby. He nodded at Cole—no need for conversation because Cole had let him know what was going on—and then he strode to the counter.

"I'm here to represent Tulip Jones."

The sheriff's lip hitched slightly. "Great. I'll take you to your client and maybe we can get this all straightened out."

Darwin wasn't happy, as the sheriff turned and let Harold through the door. It closed behind them.

Darwin turned about as pink as his shirt as he mouthed off that he was being ignored. His lawyer tapped him on the shoulder and spoke quietly, probably reminding him that the cameras were rolling.

"Turn those cameras off," he sputtered and then strode angrily toward the doors next to Cole.

Darwin paused at the door. His gaze landed on Cole and flickered over him as if he wasn't worth the dirt on the bottom of his loafers.

Cole didn't flinch or look away. He glared at Darwin, then pulled his shoulder from the wall and straightened to his full six foot two. He pushed his hat back, still holding Darwin's gaze.

The man narrowed his eyes.

Cole tucked his fingertips in his jeans pockets in order to keep himself from grabbing Darwin and throwing him out the door. He had never felt so violent in all his life.

"What are you looking at?" Darwin asked, not as belligerent as he had been.

"I don't know. I just came in out of the pasture a few minutes ago, where I was looking at a big pile of cow poop, and I don't think my view has changed much since I walked in here."

Darwin's face grew red as he glanced at the camera and realized the cameraman was still filming.

The woman with the microphone spoke into the microphone. "You're Cole Tanner, one of the Tanner billionaires from True Love."

And just like that, he was outed.

Darwin looked from the woman to Cole. "I thought you looked familiar. Why are you standing there, glaring at me and calling me names?"

"Because I'm here representing the woman, you're claiming did you an injustice."

Darwin jerked his head back. "What do you mean? How do you know Tulip?"

"I just know her, and it's none of your business. But I can assure you her story is about to come out and all these nice viewers will know exactly what you're trying to do to her. That's the head of my law team in there with her now. Sycamore and Associates—ever heard of them?" He glanced at his watch. "I'd say in about fifteen to twenty minutes, Harold Sycamore will come out of those doors with Tulip on his arm. So, hold on to your horses, pretty boy, because life's about to get real exciting."

* * *

Tulip shivered as she sat on the edge of the cot in her jail cell. She had never been in a jail cell before and she did not like it. She did not like it one bit. She felt like she was saying a nursery rhyme right there, but it was true. She did not like being in this jail cell, she did not like being called a thief; she did not like the way she felt.

But most of all, she did not like Darwin.

She was so mad at him, she would have no problem giving him a piece of her mind if she saw him.

Her gaze shifted to the mattress of the jail cell bunk. At least it didn't look terrible like in all the movies, where the mattresses didn't even have a sheet on them and were stained and grungy. This place was clean, and she planned to say a big thank-you to the nice sheriff for that. It was just the thought of being arrested and in here that had her so depressed.

No amount of clean could wash away how dirty she felt from just being here behind bars.

She thought of Cole and how he said his lawyers were on the case and one of them was on the way. She had been in here for about an hour; the sheriff had come in and assured her that they were not booking her yet. That they were waiting on her lawyer. Relief, at least in that moment, had hit her. She wasn't going to have an ugly picture taken. After all the tears she had been crying, she wiped her eyes again. She probably had mascara everywhere. She probably looked horrible. It would have been a hideous picture.

She wasn't a vain person; she just didn't want a picture like that splashed everywhere when she knew she didn't deserve it in the first place. Those pictures and records never went away. And they would affect her business. What business she would have left after running out on Darwin. She could see her whole landscaping business imploding right before her eyes. Who would want a thief coming to their property, having access to their property? The more she was thinking about it, the more she knew she was in trouble anyway because after she met Darwin, a lot of her clientele were friends of his friends. They all lived in gated communities that needed access to get into in the first place. And they were his country club buddies. She had a sinking suspicion that this was Darwin's revenge for running out on him. He was making certain she didn't have any clients left.

She swiped at a tear. She couldn't cry; she had to get a grip.

She could hear her mama's voice in her head. "Tulip Michelle Jones, you pull up your big girl panties and face this with a smile." Well, she couldn't smile, but she could pull up her big girl panties. She hadn't pulled them on lately and she needed them.

She sniffed, blinked hard, and was swiping at the tears when she heard the door opening. The sheriff stepped into the hall and a man with really shiny boots, starched jeans, and a very white starched shirt, with a very expensive-looking sports coat over the top of it and a Stetson that probably cost more than all her wardrobe in her little closet, walked in the door.

The sheriff came to her cell and inserted the key. "Your counsel is here."

She couldn't move. "Thank you. Thank you so much."

The sheriff tipped his hat as the lawyer walked into the cell. She noticed immediately that he had a kind but very strong face. His smoky-brown eyes bore into her and she could not look away. He had the kind of face that gave a person confidence that what he said was true and forthright in making people believe that he meant business.

And he was on her side. And all because of Cole.

"Tulip, I'm Harold Sycamore, and I'm here on behalf of Cole Tanner. And may I say, you've got an honorable man on your side. He's filled me in on your story. Now, let's talk and then we'll get you out of here. We'll get you bail."

She could barely speak and clasped her hands together tightly. "Thank you. I don't know what I would have done without Cole. I will work hard to pay him back for everything he's done."

"I'm sure he's not calculating. Now, let's get down to business. I have a few questions to ask you."

CHAPTER EIGHT

Two hours after he entered the building, Harold came back into the lobby where Cole was waiting, and he had Tulip with him. It took every ounce of his control not to go to her and wrap her in his arms. She looked about as dazed and confused as she had last night when he pulled her off the side of the road. He wanted to take her into his arms and hug her. But one glance toward the window where the cameras and the reporter had staked out kept him from doing that. But she was so shaken and relieved that she ran and threw her arms around his neck.

"Cole, thank you. If it wasn't for you and this nice Harold, I'd still be in there because of Darwin." She buried her face against his neck and trembled.

He couldn't help himself; he tightened his arms around her and turned her so the cameras couldn't get her face or his in the picture. Not that it would help. This picture would be plastered on the front of the tabloids tomorrow and he knew it because while he'd waited for her to get set free, more camera-carrying vultures had arrived.

Now he, Harold, and the sheriff would have to get her to his truck as the photographers got their shots of Tulip, and the reporters pelted her with questions. He could only imagine what they would be. Thankfully, as far as he could tell, Darwin had opted to leave. He had done his dirty deed—filed charges on her and then brought the paparazzi vultures to find her so they could finish off her career. The only satisfaction that Cole had was that once Darwin realized that Tulip had the power of the Tanner money behind her, he'd left.

Almost ran for his car and barely waited on his attorney to get inside.

"She was pretty shaken up." Harold did not look pleased. "We're going to have them drop these charges because she was totally set up. And she's yours to take wherever you think she wants to go. But, by the looks of what's waiting for her out those doors, I'm not advising her to go home."

Tulip lifted her head and looked at him.

"You're going to be okay," he said. "But we've got to get you to the truck and there are photographers and a reporter or two outside."

"Of course there are. I should have known he would make this a show. I've been such a fool."

He felt for her. "It's not your fault he's a jerk."

She nodded. Her gaze darted to the window.

"He wants you to be worried and embarrassed but I have a strong feeling it's going to backfire on him, so don't worry about it. And don't pay attention to them out there. We'll head out there in just a minute, but before we go I need you to tell me—are you wanting to go home?"

"I don't know what else to do. I'll just close all my windows and lock my doors. I don't even understand why they're hounding me. The same way I don't understand why Darwin did this."

"Well, for one, Darwin is a twerp. He was

embarrassed when you ran out on him, and he's getting you back for running out on him. People like him—that's how they do. But do you have somewhere else you can go?"

"I guess I could go to my mother's. But that's in Wimberly."

"That's a little out of the way for these guys, so we'll try it. I'll take you to your mother's. It will probably take a few days before they get tired of hounding you and they'll leave. Have you called your mother?"

She rubbed her temple. "I haven't. She's probably worried sick."

He hitched a brow. "She's about to find out where you're at because once you walk out that door, everyone will know where you are." Her expression crumbled. "But they're also going to know that you did not steal that car. Are you ready?"

She smiled. "I owe that to you two. So, I'm ready. Cole Tanner, I'm fully aware that if I hadn't met you, I would be sitting in this very nice sheriff's clean jail cell—and it was so clean. Thank you for being so fair to me."

The sheriff tipped his hat. He was a man of few words. "You're welcome. It was my pleasure. And may I say that I'm very glad you figured out the mistake you were making and ran out on your wedding to that fella?"

She smiled. "Me too. Okay. I'm ready."

Cole hadn't taken his arm from around her shoulders, feeling very protective of her. "Then let's go meet these wolves. Don't say anything to them. I'll warn you from experience that there's no telling what they're going to ask you." He had a bad feeling in his gut that it was not going to be what she was expecting.

Harold held the door; Cole stepped through the door first and had Tulip follow him. Harold moved in behind her so they could block her from the front and the back. The sheriff had come out and held his arms up and told the cameramen to back off. They didn't back off too much but at least they could maneuver a little.

"Cole, are you and Tulip having an affair? Is that why you broke Shelly Duncan's heart and are leaving her and her baby stranded and alone?"

It was exactly what he had expected after having seen that tabloid earlier and with Tulip telling him what it said about her having his baby. "I'm not having a baby with Shelly."

Tulip squeezed his arm but said nothing. Her eyes had gone wide.

Someone else asked a similar question and someone else pelted him with another one. The one thing about it was they weren't asking her about Darwin or the car.

"I am not involved with Shelly Duncan. We dated a brief time, and I can assure you that I am not the father of her baby, if she's actually said that—I'm not convinced you all haven't made that up."

"She said it," one of them said. "She suspected you'd found someone else and now you have Darwin Simpson's runaway bride here by your side. When did the affair begin?"

They shoved a microphone at Tulip between him and Harold, and Cole batted it out of the way, preventing the microphone from hitting her in the face. "Back off," he growled.

"Tulip, did you know he was expecting a baby with Shelly when you started having your affair with him?"

Just like he'd expected, she looked startled by the questions, never expecting this would be about him and not her. It was one thing to think you were going to face charges as a car thief—but then to find out you were being portrayed as a scheming woman sleeping with a billionaire you stole from a television talk show host? If ever there was a reality show gone bad, it was this one.

"I'm not having an affair with him. He rescued me when I wrecked my car, and he isn't the daddy to that poor baby."

He should have known she wouldn't be able to not say anything, especially when she was trying to take up for him. "I helped her out last night when she wrecked the car."

"So the public is supposed to believe that you two accidentally met up after she stole her fiancé's car."

"Ex-fiancé! And I didn't steal his car!" Her voice rose with indignation. "And he rescued me."

They'd reached the truck, and he'd lost patience. "Look, she's working for me. She's landscaping my ranch. That's it—end of the story. Now back off."

Harold stepped between them. "My clients have said all they will say for the time being."

The sheriff did the same. "Back up, folks. The show is over."

He grabbed the door handle of his truck, pulled it open and helped Tulip into the truck. Then he closed it and pushed his way through the crowd of vultures to the other side of the truck. He climbed inside, got behind the wheel, and cranked the engine. Harold stepped away from Tulip's door and he backed out slowly.

Harold was still standing guard in his rearview as Cole drove away.

Immediately, Tulip covered her face with her hands. "They think I left Darwin to have an affair with you." She lifted her head up and stared at him, her face pale. "I never saw that coming."

"That's because you're not used to this kind of junk. Sadly, since we struck oil, we've had to live with this kind of stuff. Me and all my brothers. If we lay low and keep our profiles off the grid, we can sometimes live in peace. But my stupidity at asking Shelly out brought me face-to-face with it. And it was a bad move on my part—an impulsive move that I have regretted. And I am very sorry that you had to go through that."

"It's okay. I'm just thankful that you got me out of there. Sending Harold in there—he was great. I was so scared. I have never been accused of anything like that in my life. And that Darwin, he can just take a flying leap because I'm mad. I felt bad before, but I don't anymore. What is he thinking?"

"Did you know he was there and brought the reporters to find you?"

"Darwin was here?"

"He was. I think he had hopes of getting you in front of the camera and watching the reporters eat you up."

"Well, he might have been surprised because if I had walked out that door and seen him, I might have eaten him up. I am furious at him. Putting me in that awful jail cell—although, as jail cells go, it was very nice. I'm going to send Sheriff Billings a nice thank-you card."

Cole laughed. "Tulip, you are just too nice for your own good. That will probably be the first thank-you note Sheriff Billings has ever gotten from someone who was inside his jail cells."

He could almost not hold back the laughter. What would that sheriff think when he got a nice neat little Hallmark card from Tulip? He would probably smile because he was nice and deserved something great. Cole was very glad the sheriff hadn't been like Virgil.

"Now that we're on the road, we're about to be at the crossroads, and I need to know—do you want to go to your mother's or do you want to go back to my place? I'm worried about you. And I meant it when I said you were working for me." He was startled at what he was asking. But there was just no way he could let her go back and deal with all that if she didn't think she could handle it.

"I can't come back to your place. You've already done too much and don't deserve all this."

"We'll go to your mom's and then we'll talk about it. She'll need to know what's happening."

"You're right. Oh my word, I just realized, Mama is a beautician—this could hurt her business. I have literally ruined my business with Darwin's help. Truly, everybody on my customer list and upcoming jobs has probably called in and canceled. Most likely my three weeks off is extended into forever. I can't drum up new business with all these lies about to start flying from these paparazzi. And if they show up at my mama's house, she's likely toast too."

"As bad as I hate to agree, you are probably right."

She sighed, turned her head away and stared out the passenger's side window. He saw her swipe at her eyes and knew she was trying not to cry.

"I really need a phone," she said, almost a whisper.

"I'll tell you what. We'll go by the phone store before the news gets crazy and we'll get you a new phone. Then we'll go to your mother's house."

She looked back at him. "Good idea. Then, after I see Mama, you can just drop me off at my house, and I can hole up there until this dies down. Thankfully, I have a key hidden in a planter or I'd be out of luck. Not having my purse is causing me all kinds of problems."

He didn't think that was going to work, but he let her think positive for now.

CHAPTER NINE

An hour later, Tulip called her mother on the phone that she and Cole had gotten at the phone store before anyone recognized them. They had transferred her number from her lost phone and as Cole drove toward her mother's address; she checked email and messages. Her heart sank with each one. "Well, I was right. I need to check my calendar in my database, but I'm pretty sure everyone who's on it has canceled. So anyway, I don't have to worry about that anymore."

To her surprise, Cole took one of his hands off the steering wheel, reached across, and laid his hand on her arm.

"You will be okay. And I wasn't kidding. I need my ranch—our ranch...my brothers' and mine—we need it landscaped. Where Austin and I live is the main house—that was our parents' home. Austin needs to figure out what he's going to do. Poor guy, he loves the ranch, but he loves being a physician, and he may have to get a house closer to the hospital. He just hasn't made himself do it yet. So he's bunking with me. But the deal is my parents travel all the time, but every once in a great while, they come home. And you being a landscaper got me looking around and thinking about how terrible I've let my mother's gardens start looking. So, I'll hire you right now on the spot and probably give you enough work to keep you busy for a long while. And don't worry, I have the money to do it, so that's not a problem. It's a very worthwhile expenditure."

Her stomach felt queasy. "Cole, I don't want to take advantage of you. I just feel like from the first moment you saw me walking sideways down that road with a bump on my head that I have just turned your life upside down. And then you've got this thing with Shelly. That's a lot on your plate that you're dealing with right now. You don't have to deal with me, too, especially now with all, you know, the rumors. Just because you were helping me. I feel terrible."

He slowed the truck and patted her arm and then put his hand back on the steering wheel. He turned down the road that would lead to her mother's house.

She dreaded what she would see there.

"Tulip, you can't help what happened. And, to be honest, the thing with Shelly is almost the same as the thing with you and Darwin. She is very aggressive and pretty conniving, and she wants to be Mrs. Cole Tanner. But I'm not marrying her. I can assure you, I have not slept with her, so I'm not the father of her child, if there really is one. She may just be lying. So just so you know, I'm being set up, too. And even if they hadn't connected me to you, I would still be going through the thing with Shelly. I hate that they drug you into it. But," he pulled the truck over to the side of the road and put it in park, "I'm thinking that you should probably come to the ranch. You don't even have to live in the house. The place is gated and we have some nice cabins. You can have your own little cabin. It's got a front porch with a swing—not that cowboys use that, but, well, not that people would think a cowboy uses it.

"Some of the cowboys have wives, so they enjoy the cabins. They are all scattered out—we didn't put them all together. We normally keep that one across the way open in case we have guests who need to stay over and want a little bit more privacy. So what do you think? You'd be protected—the paparazzi couldn't get to you while you're inside our gates. And you'll have a job. You might be tired of me and you might not want to be around me, and I understand that. So don't let me take over your life and have you doing things you don't want to do."

She thought about everything he said. Could she do that? Could she feel comfortable being out there on the ranch around him all the time? "Let me think about it. Let me talk to my mama. I have a message on my phone from her. She saw me on TV. And she told me—well, she just texted me; it just came through—there are cameramen in her yard."

"So what do you want to do?"

"Cole, I'll take the job. If we can, when we get

there, we'll go in and see my mama so I can give her a hug and then we'll leave and maybe make some kind of a statement that I'm not going to stay there, that I'm coming to your place or something like that."

"I get it. Yes, we can do that. If they're going to camp out at my place, they're going to drive a long way out of town and they'll be bored in no time. And Shelly—we'll just have to wait and see what she does. Maybe she'll get bored, too, now that she knows or thinks there's somebody else in the picture. They don't have to know that you're not living in my place. Now we're telling them that you're working for me, so there's no alluding that there's anything going on between us, okay? I don't want to hurt your reputation any more than this craziness going on around it has."

"Okay, but I have one more request. Can you teach me to say no? See, I can't date anybody anymore if I can't know going in that I'm going to say no if they ask me too soon to marry them or in front of a bunch of people when I know I don't need to be saying yes. I have to toughen up. And although I feel tougher right now after what Darwin did, there's no guarantee I'll be that tough if I start dating. And, to be honest, I do want to date so I can find my future husband. I do want to get married and have babies, and if I don't date, then I'm never going to find that perfect person for me."

"You have a deal. There's one thing I can do, and that's tell folks no. I'm not getting forced into anything, and Shelly's about to find that out. I don't care what goes down. It was unjust for her to accuse me of making a baby with her and walking out on it. I'm not bowing down to that because I know the truth. So, I can teach you and I'll be happy to do so."

She smiled, feeling a sense of relief just looking at him and knowing he was on her side.

What had she done to deserve Cole Tanner?

* * *

As they turned onto the street where Tulip's mother lived Cole was still thinking about the smile of relief that had bloomed across her face earlier when he'd told her he'd teach her to say no. It was the prettiest sight he had seen since he had found her on the side of the road and realized she was okay and not floating somewhere down the river. He found that he liked making her smile. And the thought that she would be at the ranch, safe and making his ranch pretty, was a good thought.

And the idea of messing with the paparazzi was a bonus to the whole situation and very, very appealing to him.

"That's Mama's house there on the right." She pointed to the white house with a wide front porch and an abundance of flowers.

"Are you sure you're ready for this?" He looked at Tulip as they pulled to a stop in front of her mother's house. Next to the house was a little building at the end of her driveway that said Mira's Beauty Palace. So it was no wonder she didn't want to stay here. With the paparazzi standing all over the driveway, people couldn't get to the door of her salon; it would ruin her business.

"I'm ready. I'll get out and hang onto your arm, and we'll barrel through them together."

He laughed. She had spunked up since they had

made the plan. He liked that. "Now that's the girl I'm glad to see again. All right, scoot over here and see if you can get out on my side." He had lifted the console between the two seats so she could scoot across the bench seat.

The paparazzi had spotted them and came running, lights flashing. He pushed the door open and waited as she scooted to the edge of the seat and hopped to the ground. She looped her arm through his, and he placed his other hand on her arm so that he could escort her in and keep her close to him. Their sides pressed close together, and he tried to ignore the warmth that filled him just at the touch of her body against his.

The questions started instantly, but he ducked his head and told them they weren't answering any questions. "The best thing y'all can do is get off the property."

Tulip walked right beside him as they walked through the group and up the steps and to the front door. When they reached the door, it opened before they could knock and Tulip led him inside.

A small, plump woman threw her arms around

Tulip. "Tulip Michelle, oh my stars! I am happy to see you."

Cole pushed the door closed behind them as Tulip and her mama hugged. They released each other. Both had tears in their eyes.

Mira dabbed at her eyes with a handkerchief. "I've been so worried. Ever since you turned and ran out of that church. But, honey, I have to tell you that I believe you made the right move."

Cole watched the exchange and was glad they'd come by here. Tulip's mother needed to see her daughter, and Tulip needed to see her mother. Tulip's gaze met his as she hugged her mother and he smiled at her, and she rewarded him with another one of her smiles. And he couldn't look away.

* * *

She smiled at Cole as her mother hugged her and he smiled back at her with eyes that seemed to reach inside of her and hug her heart tightly. The feeling stole her breath and she had to look away.

Her mother released her and dabbed at her eyes. She was so relieved that her mother was totally on her side in this.

"That man was a real donkey's behind—if you know what I mean."

Tulip chuckled. "You're right about that, Mama, and I know exactly what you're saying. I agree now. But at first, I was worried about running out and hurting him—that was before my eyes were opened to him. But I had to do it. And now his true colors have come out, and I know exactly what kind of man he is, and I'm so glad I didn't marry him."

"I can't believe he said you stole his car. The nerve of him."

"Exactly. I was in shock. And bringing the reporters to try to humiliate me was the last straw. If it hadn't been for Cole, I'd still be in that jail and he would be so happy right now."

"Thank you, Cole. For getting her out and bringing her to me."

"This is Cole Tanner, and like I said, I owe him so much. He found me last night after I had the car wreck, and he and his brother Austin, who is a doctor, took care of me. And he's been taking care of me ever since. Not only did he get me out of jail after Darwin had me thrown in there, now since Darwin has ruined my business, he's giving me a job and a place to stay on his ranch."

"What are you going to do?"

"I'm going to redo the gardens on his property. So that his mama will be pleased. And I didn't want to cause you any more pain or hurt you."

Her mama looked shocked. "You are not causing me any hardship. You can stay here. Are you sure you want to do that?"

"Yes, Mama, because you've got to have your customers and they will get tired of having to fight those people to get into the beauty shop. So if I go away, they'll leave soon. You just stay in here for a day or two and don't go outside. Then they'll leave and you can go back to your life. That's what we believe is going to happen."

"Okay, but what about him and Shelly? And the baby?" she whispered, as if Cole couldn't hear what she was saying. "Are you sure about being out there?"

"Mama, that's not true. Cole told me, and I believe him. And anyway, even if it is, that's none of my business. I'm just working at his place. I'll have my own cabin."

"Okay. But, you know, if he has a baby and he's letting that poor lady deal with it by herself—"

"Mrs. Jones, I can assure you I'm not having a baby with Shelly Duncan. You have to have relations in order for that to happen and we have not done that."

"Mama, he has to be frank like that because, well, he doesn't want you to think bad of him, and I can tell you he's telling the truth."

"Okay, I believe you because, well, you just look like a really nice guy. And if you help my Tulip like that, then you are okay in my book. But why would that woman be saying that?"

"The same reason, Mama, that Darwin is saying these things about me. It's a way to get back at somebody. Although I don't think Darwin wants me back—I think he just wants to get me back for embarrassing him. But I think Shelly is trying to get Cole to be in her life by force."

Mira huffed out an indignant breath and placed her hands on her hips. "Well, that's just terrible. You know, we have a name for people like that Shelly and it's called a hussy. That Darwin—well, I can't repeat what I want to call him right now."

Tulip laughed. "Oh, Mama. I feel terrible that we've dropped so low that we're calling people names. But I have to admit, I have a name for Darwin, too— he's a big ole jerk."

Mira hitched a brow over stern eyes. "I guess we'll go with your name for him. And after he sent you to jail, I don't feel the least bit sorry for dropping low. Though maybe after I calm down, I'll let the good Lord set me straight. Right now, you two are coming to the kitchen and having some cookies and coffee. We're going to sit down and talk and we're going to ignore that stuff happening outside that door. Oh, and I have your purse, Tulip. After you ran out I went to the dressing room and grabbed it and all of your other things. Thought you probably weren't going to want to go back there, you know."

"Oh mama," Tulip threw her arms around her

mother and hugged her tight. "I never even thought about you doing that. Thank you so much. I guess I didn't need a new phone after all."

Mira smiled brightly. "Nope, you did not and you are so welcome. Now, come on, I want to know everything there is to know, not that I'm going to talk about it or anything, I promise you. But you know when all my customers come in here, they're going to be so excited and want some details. Especially because, well, Cole, you are good-looking. And a billionaire. Not that it matters to me. People are people and money makes no difference to me, but I will just tell them the truth and say you are not the father and you are not going back to her and that my baby did not break y'all up."

Her mother was so going to talk about it despite her promise. She couldn't help herself and Tulip knew this. Better she had as much truth as possible. She was glad when Cole looked at the ceiling, shook his head and then laughed.

"Mira, you can tell your ladies whatever you want. Just as long as you make sure they know your daughter is okay."

Mira hugged him around the waist. "Thank you, Cole Tanner. I think I'm going to adore you." She peeked out the corner of the window and frowned. "I'm going to get my shotgun after those reporters if they don't stop stepping on my rhododendrons and my lilies of the valley."

Tulip grimaced, meeting Cole's look of alarm. "God's going to have to forgive her, because she takes her rhododendrons seriously."

"Mira, please don't go out there with your shotgun. I'll personally buy you new rhododendrons, but it won't be good for anyone if you step out on that porch and start threatening reporters with a shotgun. It won't do me or you any favors, but it will especially not help your daughter."

"Then I'll keep my shotgun in the house. But I might get a broom after them."

CHAPTER TEN

When they got up to leave, Cole felt much better. Mira was a very refreshing and entertaining lady, and he had thoroughly enjoyed himself. He and Tulip were both being hugged like there was no tomorrow from Mira when he realized there was some sort of commotion going on outside the door.

Mira did, too, and she hustled over to the window and peeked through the screen. "Oh my stars." She hurried to the front door, yanked it open and stepped out onto the porch before Cole could stop her.

He stepped out behind her, and Tulip followed. All the reporters had gone to the end of the driveway where there was a short, squat, little lady with curly gray hair that was tinged slightly blue; she had her hands on her hips and was just talking away to the reporters.

Mira stepped to the edge of the porch. "Beulah Anne, get yourself in here and stop talking to those reporters."

The lady looked toward Mira, waved, and then—giving a big nod of her head and looking quite indignant—she barreled her way through the reporters to the porch.

"Now, Mira, they were just yacking away, and I was just coming to see who in the world or what in the world had happened to your Tulip. I saw the news, and I had to come see for myself and…and, that, that is Cole Tanner standing right there in the flesh. Oh no, it's true. Tulip Michelle Jones, did you break him and Shelly Duncan up? Are the rumors true?"

Mira grabbed Beulah Anne's arm and tugged her into the house, and Tulip gave Cole a roll of the eyes. They followed both of them inside as the reporters continued to call out questions. Cole glared at them then slammed the door, drowning them out.

Inside, Beulah Anne had put her hand on her very endowed bosom and was breathing hard as she stared at Cole and then looked at Tulip. "I was standing right out there with those reporters telling them that not a word that they were saying was true. But I just thought that they were mistaken. Surely, Tulip, you're not a homewrecker?"

Mira looked very insulted. "Now, Beulah Anne, if you're going to keep insulting my daughter like that, I'm going to have to ask you to leave. You know, Tulip Michelle—she would not do such a thing."

"Well, two days ago I would have believed you, but then she ran out on that young man of hers and just broke his heart right there in front of all of us, so I frankly don't know what to think about your Tulip now."

Tulip laid a hand on Beulah Anne's arm and very gently spoke. "Now, Beulah Anne, you know that I wouldn't do that and, yes, I can totally understand how it can be very confusing. But the reporters can take the news and twist it and turn it however they want to. And over the coming days, you're going to hear all kinds of things about me and Cole. However, I can assure you that whatever you hear about Cole is not true. He is the nicest, hunkiest, wealthy guy I have ever in my life been around, and he rescued me. So you just keep that in mind and be assured that he's not having a baby with Shelly Duncan. And he did not just up and leave her to raise a baby by herself. That's all tabloid gossip—you know how they just want to sell a magazine and entertain. No telling what you're going to be reading about me and him over the next few days since I'm going to be working for him."

Beulah Anne's face grew tense. "You mean to tell me they're just flat out lying about y'all?"

"Yes, ma'am, they are."

"Well, I do not like a liar. The next one of them who shoves a microphone in my face is probably going to get a knee in the you-know-where—I learned that in my self-defense class and have been wondering when I was going to get to practice. And I assure you that I will spread the word that what's in those tabloids is all false about y'all. But why would that Shelly Duncan be lying like that?"

Mira and Tulip both turned and looked at Cole. Cole's eyes narrowed as they stared at him; both of them crossed their arms and then turned back to Beulah Anne.

Tulip was the first one to smile and gave him a wink as she said, "Now, Beulah Anne, like I said, Cole's the nicest, hunkiest, wealthy dude I know, and Shelly Duncan has not been blind about that fact, and she just wants him however she can get him—even if it is by lying. And he won't say this but I will: if she is having a baby, well then, we don't even know who it belongs to."

Beulah Anne's mouth had fallen open and then she snapped it shut and gave him a very sympathetic look.

That almost made him chuckle, but he was just in shock by the way that Mira and Tulip were looking at him. But he was going to eventually have to get used to the fact that he was a nice, hunky, wealthy guy or dude or whatever they were calling him. Boy, had he gotten into an alternate universe or something. "Ladies, I'd rather just be known as a nice guy. You can leave off the wealthy and the hunky part."

"And see there? That's just like I told you, Beulah Anne," Mira said. "He's just the nicest thing. And I adore him and I've only known him for a very little while."

"And I adore you, too, Mira. But I believe now that we've gotten Beulah Anne away from the wolves out there that Tulip and I need to head out. So, Beulah Anne, do you need to leave with us or will you be okay when it's time for you to go home if they're still out there?"

Beulah Anne gave him a very smug look. "Now that I know they're the vultures and they're full of lies, I can handle them. Although I will do my best not to embarrass Tulip if they put me on the news. Speaking of putting me on the news—Mira, how does my hair look?"

On that note, Cole held his arm out and Tulip slipped her arm through his. "We're going to head out ahead of you, Beulah Anne." They hugged and said good-bye; he got engulfed in tight hugs from both ladies. He had to bend down in order for them to reach around his neck but he hugged them back. They were on Tulip's side and that meant a lot to him.

The moment they stepped out onto the porch, the questions started flying again.

"Are you moving in with him?" one of the reporters asked Tulip as they pushed their way down the steps.

"I am not moving in with Cole. We are just friends. Actually, he's my employer. I'm about to start redoing all of his gardens at his house. Just like he said to some other reporter a little while ago. Now, my mother really likes her rhododendrons and her lilies of the valley, so I would suggest you quit stomping all over them."

More questions came but, he and Tulip said nothing else. He reached his truck, yanked open the door, and she climbed in. He moved in right behind her; she scooted over to her side, and he closed the door.

But a reporter got a microphone in right before he got the door closed.

"Cole Tanner, what are you going to do about your baby with Shelly? Are you just going to abandon it?"

"I will repeat: I am not the father of Shelly Duncan's baby. You'll have to take that up with Shelly." Then he yanked his door closed, and the reporter got his hand out just in the nick of time.

* * *

Tulip breathed a sigh of relief as they drove away from her mother's house. Then saw in the rearview as several jumped into their vehicles and started following them.

"I was afraid of that," Cole said as he drove with one hand as he slipped his Bluetooth earpiece on. "I need to make a call."

"Sure," she said, distracted as she watched the cars following them.

He called out the name Luke Despain and after a moment he said, "Luke, hey buddy, it's Cole Tanner. Yeah, been awhile. Look, I'm on my way out of Wimberly and I've got a host of reporters following me and we're heading in your ranch's direction. Are you home?"

She listened to his end of the conversation and was a bit confused by it.

"Fifteen minutes at most." Cole's lip hitched into a smile. "Sounds good, Luke. I'll owe you." Cole laughed then. "Yeah, I figured this would make your day. Have a ball. Talk to you soon. I'll wave at you as we pass by."

She was very curious about what he and this Luke had planned. "What was that about?"

He turned down the main road that was a turnoff into her mother's neighborhood and then gassed it. He shot through a yellow light just before it turned red.

To her surprise, three stinking cars ran the red light. "They ran the red light."

"Those people are just crazy. It's a wonder they didn't kill somebody." He frowned into the rearview.

She sighed. "They have been the cause of killing people. Princess Diana and others. It's terrible."

He reached out and covered her hand with his. "True, but today they're going to get stopped. Give me a few minutes to get out of town and they won't be following us anymore today. That's what the call was about."

His hand was warm and reassuring, 'So, what's happening?" she asked.

He smiled. "Have some patience." He grinned and then winked.

She felt some of the tension inside of her lessen. Cole had it under control. Cole seemed to always have things under control, and it was a reassuring trait. Whether he really did or not, he made sure she felt like he did. And it worked to help her calm down, which was very welcome today.

Fifteen minutes later, he pulled his hand from Tulip's and put it back on the steering wheel as they approached a ranch with a sign that said Despain Ranch.

There was a man sitting on a horse, and a couple of others in an ATV. Behind them was a herd of cows, flanked by more cowboys on horses.

"What are they doing?" she asked. They looked like they were ready and waiting for something.

"That's Luke and his ranch hands." Cole waved at him as he drove the truck past the group. "Watch through the back window if you want. It's going to be quite a show."

Tulip turned so she could see through the back window. "Those cows are going across the road and they're stopping." She laughed. "Nobody could get through there now."

She stared at him and he grinned at her. "It will be awhile before they get through. Luke will hold them off as long as he can until traffic stacks up. Which is the reason we came this way—it's not on the beaten track and doesn't have a lot of traffic."

"Great. You lost them."

"They know where we live and they'll get to the ranch, eventually. It's just fun to make life harder for them. Plus, it'll give us time to get in the gate. We'll be settled in behind the fences and everything will be fine."

"That sounds good. I'm sick of them and I enjoyed that as much as you and your friend did. But I do hope that they get tired and go away soon."

"They will."

She considered her words carefully. "But what about Shelly? That story will still be alive even after mine dies. And it seems that's what they're focused on." She worried it wouldn't go away as easily as her car-thieving, runaway bride story rose and fizzled in the dust of his mounting scandal.

"Manufactured scandal. Harold is contacting Shelly's camp as we speak. A little cease and desist. She's just trying to see what she can get. After contact with Harold, she will stand down. I hope that doesn't make you think I'm a terrible person."

"No. If the baby's not yours and she's just trying to do this to entrap you into marrying her, then you have nothing to feel bad about and I don't hold anything against you. I don't care if it's a man or a woman—if one party is lying, it's wrong. You know, that's one of the things about all this women's movement—believe me, I'm all for women not getting stepped on and getting their rights and being believed, but every woman who falsely accuses a man of something like this is hurting the women who have true stories that need to be heard. I just despise when women hurt other women by lying like that."

"It happens both ways. I don't like it when men mistreat women. That's why I'm having such a great time taking care of you right now. But on that same note, I don't like trying to be trapped. So, we'll be letting her know that if she really is having a baby, I'm demanding a paternity test the moment the baby is born. Just to clear my name. She knows I'm not the daddy, so that right there will hopefully fix the lie."

She felt bad for him. Relief washed over her as he slowed and turned in to the drive to his ranch. She'd seen it all that morning and after realizing this was a billionaire's ranch, she hadn't thought anything of the huge iron gates and stone entrance and black pipe fencing. Now, as he pushed a button on his dashboard and the gates opened, she spotted the security cameras trained on them as they entered. She had a feeling there were more around that she couldn't see.

"Every entrance of this ranch and every other ranch we own has similar setups. This is one reason I wanted you to come back with me. The landscaping job offer just popped into my thoughts automatically, but it's perfect. You'll be safe here until all this ridiculousness smooths over."

* * *

Tulip stared at the cute little house that Cole had pulled up in front of. It was a log cabin, but it had a stone fireplace on one end, and it had a front porch and a red swing—a double seater—hanging on the porch. She immediately got a vision of sitting on that porch, cuddled up with a blanket and drinking her morning coffee, listening to the sounds of the ranch waking up. And right after that vision, she got another one of cuddling up with Cole in that blanket, listening to the sounds of the evening.

She put the brakes on that vision immediately. She was out here to work and to hide out, and the last thing she needed to do was let this growing crush—infatuation—she had with the man get out of hand. He didn't deserve her causing him that kind of trouble. No, she was just going to draw him up some plans for some enhancements to the patios they already had; she could envision a gazebo. His mother had planted some great flowers; she had some she wanted to add to it, and they needed some TLC. They had been neglected. All of his knockout roses that had been planted needed to be dead-headed—they needed all those little blooms that had died and had been left on the vine clipped right off. That was a time-consuming project, but one that was very much needed in order for those red roses to bloom in abundance. She personally loved doing that—dead-heading on those roses—when she was upset. Nothing like clipping the bud off a rose to take out your anger on.

Dead-heading a rosebush was so much better than giving in to temptation of getting on social media and letting her anger hang out for everyone to see. Thankfully, there were a lot of roses on the property that needed clipping. She saw promise in the work, but also in the landscaping. Red roses and yellow lantana flowers at their bases was a beautiful combination along the edges of the cabin.

She looked at Cole. "This is adorable. This is where I'm going to live?"

"That's what I was thinking. If you like it. You're welcome to take the room in the house where you were last night, but I thought this would be better. Give you more privacy."

"Oh no, I love this. Me being out here will be

perfect. I'll be out of y'alls way—y'all can go about your business as usual. And for now, this will be my home office. I cannot wait to get started on landscaping all of this. You just have to tell me what you want, where you want it, and where to start. I tend to be pretty extravagant sometimes on what I create, especially around pools, and I saw you have a pool back there. Do you swim?" She did not picture Cole Tanner as a guy who lounged in a pool, but maybe he swam laps... Still, he was a cowboy through and through, and swimming laps didn't fit him.

"I've been known to swim, but in the lakes here on the ranch. The pool was my mom's, who would not be caught dead swimming in a lake."

"I totally agree with her. I've never gone swimming in a lake."

"Now, come on, you don't know what you're missing. There is nothing like on a hot day in Texas to dive into the cool lake water fed into by a cold creek."

"You make it sound tempting."

"You hang with me, and I'll have you taking a dip before you know it."

Butterflies lifted through her at the very tempting idea of swimming with Cole.

They got out of the truck and walked up the steps. She walked over to the swing and pushed it. It was inviting. She ignored the flash of the vision of her and Cole snuggled up on it again. She was going to have to stop that.

Cole opened the door and pushed it open, and she walked inside. The cabin was as cute inside as it was outside. The stone fireplace had a lovely hearth. It was decorated in reds, tans, and blues, and was just beautiful.

But the cabinets in the small kitchen were gorgeous.

"Did you build this?"

"I helped the guy who built this cabin. This was the first one that we built, and I learned to build cabinets and things while I helped him build the cabins on this ranch. That's where I got my love of it."

She ran her hand along the smooth edge of the wood. "You had a great teacher because these are beautiful."

"Thanks. He did most of the work on these cabinets because, like I say, I was really raw when we worked on these cabinets. But I learned a lot watching him work on these. The last few cabins that are here, I did most of the work on the cabinets. He cut me loose so I could show him what I could do and I had a great time. There are several cabins."

She turned slowly, looking at the lovely little room. "Well, I'm going to enjoy this retreat."

"Great. Now let's go over to the house and grab a bite to eat, get you some sleepwear and toothbrush and whatever else you need for the night. We'll sneak out tomorrow and get you some clothes and anything else you need. I'm sure after the day you've had, you're ready to rest."

"I am. But a soak in that beautiful claw-footed tub is going to be heavenly."

CHAPTER ELEVEN

Cole was going crazy. Three days after having moved Tulip into the guesthouse, things had calmed down some outside the gates of the ranch. His lawyer had served notice to Darwin that he could continue or reap the consequences of trying to hurt Tulip—and face a deep-pocketed investigation into his business dealings, which he showed the man a preliminary report that Cole's investigator, Jensen had uncovered with minimum effort.

Darwin had quietly withdrawn his charges within the hour.

Cole hadn't been worried about Darwin; he was small potatoes. Shelly Duncan, on the other hand, hadn't decided what she was going to do. Harold had called and said that she was still maintaining that Cole was the daddy of her baby. Cole knew this would have been a miracle as he had not slept with the woman. He hated being raked through the coals for something he hadn't done, and then he hated that Shelly had done this. They hadn't been compatible; they both had different life goals, but he hadn't pinned her as a person who would try to trick a guy into marrying her. It was confusing, and he hadn't figured out how he was going to deal with it. He was probably going to have to go see her and talk about this face-to-face.

But none of that was what was making him crazy. It was staring out his office window and watching Tulip at work. He was infatuated with the woman. She'd dived into making over his yard with the enthusiasm of a woman obsessed. It was clear she lived and breathed landscaping flowers and rocks. For the first couple of days, she had cut the old blooms off his mother's many rosebushes and she'd done it with diligence. She'd told him it was therapy.

She'd gotten a lot of therapy, if that was the case. He'd told her whatever she needed, it was at her disposal and today she had asked for rocks.

145

"Rocks?" he'd asked, chuckling at her seriousness.

"Yep, rocks about thigh-high and some about knee-high." She'd smiled, squinting slightly in the sunlight.

She'd been so cute, he'd had a hard time listening to her words. "Sure thing."

"Great. This is going to be good."

She'd spun away and walked off, intent on her work, and he'd just stood there for the longest moment, like an adolescent with a crush. Then he'd come inside and ordered the lady her rocks. Rocks were native to the Hill Country landscape, and plentiful, and they were being delivered tomorrow after lunch.

So far, she was doing all the work herself and said when she needed help, she would let him know and then he could bring in some of his ranch hands to help. But right now she needed the output of energy that it gave her, which he understood, and she had buried herself in dirt, digging and planting—replanting was what she was doing.

He liked watching her work. She would stand with her hands on her hips and study an area and he would wonder what she was seeing. Then, after she studied it for a minute, she would get to work. And like she said, there was so much digging and moving around he had no clue what she was doing, but she looked great doing it. Tulip Jones in shorts and tank top, all tanned and sleek-muscled with her cascading hair and content expression, was a distraction he could not look away from. She was working while Cole could barely get any work done.

There was a knock at his office door. "Come in," he called, knowing the only person in the house was Rose, his housekeeper. She'd come to work yesterday for her four days a week, and she and Tulip had gotten along instantly, as if they had known each other forever.

He spun around in his chair to stare at his computer screen, hitting the button to make the screen come alive.

Rose poked her head inside. "Cole, I was wondering if you want a refill on your unsweet tea?"

"How'd you read my mind? I was just sitting here thinking about unsweet tea."

She laughed and came in. "Well, good. Actually, I'm using the tea as an excuse. I've been watching that Tulip and she is a hard worker. I like her."

"I believe she likes you, too. You two act like you've known each other for forever."

Rose poured tea into his glass. "We're both down-to-earth people, you know what I mean?"

"I do."

"How do you like Tulip, Cole?"

He had known Rose a long time and now looked at her with a bit of wariness. "I like her a lot. Why are you wondering?"

Rose laughed. "Cole Tanner, I might be several decades older than you but that doesn't mean I can't see. I never did think you dating that Shelly Duncan was going anywhere because she just wasn't right for you. But Tulip is a different story. When she came in for breakfast, I saw very clear interest in your eyes. Why aren't you going over there and inviting her to dinner or something?"

"Because…" It was actually a good question—one that he hadn't really faced up to yet.

"Because what? Because nothing. Here's my idea. Since you do have all those irritating camera people hanging around at the gate—thank goodness there were fewer this morning when I arrived—I'm going to cook a really nice meal tonight and leave it in the warming drawer. I'm going to set a lovely table on the patio, and you can ask her over for a date. It will just be you and her—I know Austin is working at the hospital for the next three days. And your other brothers are not coming over while those cameras are out there. It will be a perfect date night."

"Now, Rose, when I get ready to date, I don't need you helping me out."

She set the tea pitcher on the desk and crossed her arms. "I beg to differ. I think that if you planned to ask her out, you would have done it. I'm not sure what's holding you back, but I figure you need a little nudge or kick in the pants. Don't let this thing that Shelly's doing to you hold you back from a good thing. And, yes, I know about Shelly and this baby. It's all over the tabloids, but I also heard through my niece, who knows the lady who does Shelly's hair. She told her hairdresser that you were the daddy of her baby."

"It's not true—"

"Oh, I know that. You would never run out on your responsibility. So, I didn't believe a word of it. But that's neither here nor there right now. The fact is that you're getting the raw end of the deal on that, but you shouldn't let that cause you to miss out on what could be the best thing to ever happen to you. I haven't seen you interested in a woman in a while. You know, you were basically bored out of your mind, and I think that's why you asked Shelly out. But when you look at Tulip out there, you brighten up. And if your mother was here, she would be excited. Well, anyway, here soon, you march out there and you ask that woman to dinner. I'll have it ready when I leave, so then it's up to you." She winked and headed toward the door. "You've always been a smart man."

He chuckled as she left the room. She was something.

While he had been sitting in here, dragging his feet, Rose said what he needed to hear. She absolutely right. He was going to dinner with Tulip…if she agreed.

* * *

Tulip stared at her reflection in the bathroom mirror and tried to quell the nerves radiating through her. She'd had nervous butterflies when she was around Cole, but tonight was different because he'd asked her to dinner.

Since moving into the cabin and beginning work on the gardens, she'd tried very hard to keep her mind off him in any other capacity than her boss, and the nice guy who'd rescued her. But it hadn't been working very well. And she'd sensed when they were talking that he was maybe experiencing the same issues. But she'd thought maybe she had just been wishing his interest into existence.

They had gone out a back way the morning after she'd moved into the cabin, and he'd taken her shopping. They'd both worn hats and had managed not to draw attention from anyone. She'd been thankful to know that not everyone paid attention to the tabloids, nor did they care about drawing them out when they did recognize them. They'd just stowed her new clothes in the truck when Harold had called and said Darwin had dropped all charges and wouldn't bother her anymore. At the news, without thinking, she had thrown her arms around Cole's neck and held on tight as she'd told him thank you several times.

When his arms had tightened around her, her arms had tightened around him and she'd wanted to kiss him. The realization had her yanking out of his arms and, from then until now, fighting not to get carried away with the emotions she felt for him.

She stared at her reflection, smoothed the skirt down of her soft green-toned sundress and wondered what she was going to do. She had just gotten out of two different bad situations, so what was she doing?

Feeling more excited about a dinner than she'd ever felt before.

Sucking in a long, slow breath, she walked toward the door of the cabin, opened it, and stepped out onto the porch. When Cole had strode out of the house earlier that day, she had her hands in the dirt and she'd thought he'd come to give her an update on the rocks she'd asked him to order. And he had done that, letting her know it was on its way. Then he'd asked her to dinner on the deck, with a special meal prepared by Rose.

She had no idea what was going to happen tonight, whether she would be able to work with him tomorrow or not. But, then again, she would have to face that moment when it came. She walked down the steps and started across the parking area. She could see he was moving around on the patio and saw him light a flame. He was lighting candles.

Anticipation filled her. She was halfway across the rock when he came to meet her. The man looked amazing. He had on a black button-up shirt—probably a Western one. When she got close to him, she would see jeans that fit him to perfection. His belt buckle flashed in the late afternoon light and he had on dress boots, not his dusty work boots that she'd been seeing him in the last few days. This was indeed a date.

He smiled as she got closer. She stopped walking. He stopped walking two feet from her. Oh, she could have thrown herself into his arms at that very moment. It was a terrible thing to have to keep her feet latched to the ground.

"I think I might be a smidge early."

"Yes, you are. I was going to walk over there and escort you to dinner, but this is fine. You look beautiful."

Her heart did a little kerthunk. "Thank you. And you look very handsome."

He held out his arm; she put hers through it and they walked across the gravel together.

* * *

Rose had prepared his favorite, which was her cheesy enchiladas—they were amazing—and a salad and a deep-dish okra casserole. Texas down-home comfort food—nothing over-the-top fancy, which he suspected was her signaling that she knew Tulip was a good, down-to-earth woman. He held the chair as soon as they walked onto the patio and over to the table. "Everything's done. All you need to do is sit down and enjoy. This is Rose's specialty and my favorite, which I had no influence on. I had no idea what she was going to fix but I approve wholeheartedly." All he had to do was carry the dishes out from the warming drawer.

Tulip smiled, looking at the table. "It looks yummy. And I'm a big fan of enchiladas myself."

She moved past him to sit down in the chair, and he caught a whiff of sweet florals that had him wanting to lean forward as she took the seat and bury his nose into her pretty cinnamon-colored waves. But he didn't. His hands flexed on the chair as he scooted it forward and he told himself to just take it easy and enjoy the evening. And he was going to do that, that was for certain.

It was a round table with four chairs, so he sat in the chair in the pie shape next to hers, not across from hers. That was exactly how Rose had set up the table and exactly how he wanted it; he didn't want a whole table between them. And that position across from her was where the full tea pitcher was set and a pitcher of water with lemon. "We have wine, if you'd like a glass."

"No, thank you. I'll be just fine with tea, please."

He reached for the pitcher and then poured the tea

into her glass. He liked having something to do as his brain flew with trying to figure out what to talk about.

She looked beautiful. His heart had started pounding in his chest when he had looked across the yard and spotted her coming his way. The soft green sundress brought out the green in her eyes and the skirt of it fluttered around her thighs. Her skin had turned to a golden tan in the sunlight, even more so than normal. It was easy to tell that she worked in the sunshine most of the time. "You haven't burned." That was the way he started the conversation.

She smiled. "I know—it's a miracle. I got my skin tone from my father. He died when I was younger, but he had Italian in him. So, I have a combination of my mother's Irish background and my father's Italian olive skin, so anyway, the combination worked for me. Especially seeing what I do. I try not to get too much sun, but thankfully I don't burn like I could if I only had my mother's Irish background. Although I know a lot of people with Irish backgrounds who tan beautifully but not often and I'm not a pro on the subject but red hair, you know, does tend to be more delicate in the sunshine normally." She laughed. "I guess you can tell I'm a little bit nervous. I talk too much when I'm nervous."

On impulse, he reached over and laid his hand on hers. He squeezed gently. "I'll be honest, too. I'm a little nervous myself. I'm kind of worried about asking you on a date like this because, well, you know, you're working for me and you're trapped out here. If you don't want to say yes to a date, you're not going to hurt my feelings, okay? Do we understand that?"

She stared at him. Her expression softened into a very gentle one that twisted at his heart.

"Thank you. Speaking of, one of our agreements was that you would teach me how to say no, even in uncomfortable situations. I'm going to hold you to that, you know."

He smiled and after another gentle squeeze of her hand, he pulled his away and reached for the tongs to the salad bowl. "Don't worry, that is high on my agenda. I just wanted you to get settled before we started having our tutoring classes."

She laughed, and he did too.

"Salad?"

She held her plate out to him in answer and he put a nice big helping of salad onto her salad plate.

"It's got all the fresh stuff in it. Rose has that garden out back—I don't know if you've noticed it. She loves that garden. She has one at home, too; she insists on here and there. She has a green thumb. I bet you do, too."

"I noticed the garden, and I wondered, because there is a difference between how that garden looks and how these flowers look. I thought something was up."

"Now you know. Rose doesn't have time to take care of the flowers with keeping us guys straight and, you know, cleaned up. But she insists on the garden and we have it fixed up where there are no weeds in the container box back there."

"Well, that's good. So are you starting to worry about what I'm doing in your yard?"

He put salad on his plate and then set the tongs down as he hitched a brow. "Well, I have noticed that you've left some holes in some places and things are rearranged, so I'm interested."

"Well, tomorrow, if the rocks are here, we're going to have some fun. I have it all drawn out in my—I was going to say my office, but in the cabin and I'll show it to you. I have it in my brain, but you'll want to see it. I think it's going to be awesome. And, uh, I think your mother will like it. It's in the same general vein of what your mother did but I kind of have, you know, a more out-of-the-box flair—I can't help myself. You told me to go for it, and so I am. But this is essentially your garden now. See," she toyed with the salad as her eyes held his, dancing with excitement, "because of that, because it's a, you know, a guy's garden, I've made it more—or I'm about to make it more—a little manly. It's still going to be beautiful and the flowers she loves will still be there, but I'm adding elements that make it more solid, you know?"

He forked some salad. "And there comes the rocks—I get it. I'm looking forward to seeing what you do."

"Great."

They ate and chatted about the gardens. She asked

about his family and he told her about his brothers—how Bret was a bull rider on the PBR circuit and had been a National Rodeo Finals Champion two years in a row a couple of years back and was home on occasion but that he loved what he did and left the ranching up to him, Levi, and Jake, and how Austin was, as she knew, the physician who barely had time to eat and sleep at home before doing what he loved—taking care of sick people and helping people not to get sick.

He asked about her dad and how they'd lost him to illness when she was young and how that had affected her. How she had always envied people who had fathers and mothers. But she had been very grateful for the years she had had with her dad and she had great memories. He liked that about her; she seemed so solid and on such good footing about everything in her life, except where it came to saying no to guys who obviously tried to take advantage of her sweetness.

As they were finishing up the enchiladas, he vowed to himself that before she left his ranch, he would make sure that she didn't get conned by another man. As he went in the house and pulled out the cherry cream cheese pie that Rose had made—again, his favorite—and carried it out to present to Tulip, he had to fight the sudden longing in his own heart that maybe there was actually something brewing between him and Tulip. He would have to be careful about that. She worked for him; he had rescued her, and she was actually a little bit trapped out here. And he would not take advantage of that.

CHAPTER TWELVE

The sound of a bullfrog in the distance and farther past the familiar sounds of coyotes' singing at the full moon serenaded them as they reached Tulip's cabin later that evening.

"It's so lovely tonight," Tulip said as she and Cole reached the steps to the cabin. "I enjoyed dinner very much." Cole had been an absolute gentleman, catering to her in every way. The man was as genuine as he seemed—no inkling of pretentiousness, which she'd had to tolerate when she'd been with Darwin. Why had she been a weakling and continued dating the guy? And then allowed him to play to her sympathetic side and agree to marry him?

Dinner with Cole had highlighted all that was right

in how a real man treated a lady and shined light on all the wrong ways Darwin treated her…and probably every other woman he'd ever dated. Cole was the real deal.

"The meal was so delicious. So down-to-earth."

He smiled as he lifted a strand of her hair and caressed it between his fingers. "Rose fixed all my favorites."

Which he had told her as they were eating, and it was almost as if Rose had been signaling to Tulip that Cole might be a billionaire, but he had no arrogance about him. He did not put on airs and liked simple things. Tulip had noticed and she loved that about him.

When he had covered her hand with his at the beginning of the meal, her heart had begun to pound and her knees went weak. Thankfully, she'd been sitting down or she might have had to cling to him to remain standing. The very idea was appealing.

But she couldn't let her emerging feelings for Cole show too much. They were, after all, client and boss and she was living here to do a job. Not ogle him.

Even though he had promised that he would make

sure she could say no to guys who tried to con her into marrying them, she hoped with all of her heart that he didn't think that included him.

It was a very eye-opening hope that she was almost afraid to let grow inside her heart. But she knew, even with as little as she had known him over this last week, that she was in very serious, deep waters because he was exactly the kind of man she could really fall for. And it didn't take months of dating to know that.

And yet she didn't want him to feel as though he owed her anything because she was here. Now, looking at him—leaned back against the porch post and holding the strand of hair in his fingertips—she was struck by his eyes that glowed golden in the moonlight as he studied her.

She couldn't move and she wished—yes, she did—that he would kiss her. She hadn't felt so strongly about wanting a kiss in her life.

"I like your hair. It's pretty, just like you."

"Thank you. I'm always amazed at how hot it can get when I'm working. Sometimes I think I need to cut it off—you know, get it off my neck—and I wouldn't have to worry about all this thickness in the heat of the summer."

He let go of her hair and rested his hand on her hip, sending heat swelling through her as he tugged her slightly toward him. She went willingly, with a pounding heart.

"Don't do that." His voice was silken. "It's too pretty to cut, although that's your decision. But it would be a shame."

Her skin burned through the material of her dress where his hand rested on her hip. She leaned toward him, wishing… "I haven't been able to bring myself to do it. I'm probably not going to since I know you like it." There—how blunt could that be?

His lip curled upward as he straightened, no longer leaning against the post, and that brought them to where they were a breath apart. His gaze rested on her lips and in response, she licked her bottom lip. He leaned in and kissed her.

She melted as his lips claimed hers, and his hand on her hip slid to her back. He shifted slightly, and she settled against him. Her arms settled around his neck, where they longed to be. Where they belonged—oh, what a thought.

His other hand moved to cup the back of her head as the kiss lengthened. Her world spun out of control and Tulip was free-falling—and then the kiss ended.

"I better go home," he said, though his eyes continued to drink her in. "I'm overstepping my boundaries."

Boundaries. She was breathing heavily as he stepped back from her; he, too, was breathing heavier than before.

His eyes flashed in the porch light. "I will have to be careful around you, Tulip Jones. You are very tempting."

Her insides melted at that. Maybe there was hope between them. "You are, too. We may have a problem."

"I believe you're right. I'm supposed to be teaching you to say no, not wanting to nibble on your lips."

"I'm not complaining but I feel weird saying that.

We need to be careful. I don't want you to think I'm trying to move out here on your property and trick you or anything. You've got a lot on your plate with everything that's going on with you."

He took a step back. "I don't think I'm worried at all about you trying to take advantage of me. It's me mixing you up. That being said, before I stick my boot in my mouth or mess up anymore, I'm going to head home. If you need anything, you've got my number. Good night, Tulip Jones."

Her heart pounded, and she had the strongest urge to cross the space between them, to throw her arms back around his neck and never let go. "Good night, Cole Tanner. Sleep well."

He laughed, turned, and as he walked away, said over his shoulder, "I doubt that's going to happen."

She smiled, loving that answer. She was in the same predicament as he was and it felt very good knowing he felt the same.

* * *

They worked hard over the next few days. The woman

could work like a cowboy when it came to dealing with the heat and working until the job was done. He practically had to make her stop for lunch over the next few days. She had shown him the designs, and he liked what she was doing.

The gardens would have more of a Hill Country/South Texas feel with bolder plants and those that would be found growing wild in Hill Country versus the strictly flowering flowers that his mother had loved. The ones that Tulip was planting would require less maintenance and the sprinkler system would take care of the ones his mother had planted. Tulip just made them easier to handle, and some of them that had needed transferring, she had moved to their own little garden that would be flooded with sprinkler system water and need less maintenance.

They moved rocks and put them together, deciding together the placement and appeal. It was sweaty work, and she didn't seem to care in the least. The woman loved what she did.

He had to watch her closely or she would try to move boulders that he had trouble rolling around. He'd been adamant in telling her to back off and not hurt herself. She'd been just as adamant a couple of times, reminding him that this was her business and she knew how to move a rock. "You're not moving the big ones when I'm around and I mean it, Tulip." He'd finally had to set the law down. "My property, my rules."

"Fine. But that just means you will have to tag along beside me instead of getting your work done in your office."

He'd grinned, tugged her into his sweaty arms, and kissed her. "Exactly what I was hoping you would say."

She'd laughed, and they'd kissed long and deep, right there in the middle of the yard for anyone to see. It wasn't until later he'd realized a cameraman standing on the top of a van could have gotten a shot of them. But he was too long gone and involved in loving the feel of her in his arms and the taste of her lips to care.

* * *

When Austin finally got off duty from his stint at the

hospital three days later, he'd gotten out of his truck and walked over to them with an expression of complete disbelief.

"This is amazing. I've been gone for three days and it looks like I've been gone for a month. I bet this took all the ranch hands to get this done."

"No, just one determined mastermind pushing me to work harder." Cole laughed and Tulip's eyes twinkled as she took his playful barb.

Austin looked from her to Cole. "Looks like you two had fun working with each other, and it shows."

"We did." Tulip smiled and looked around. "It has turned out better than I envisioned and I'm glad you noticed."

Austin hitched a brow at him while Tulip wasn't watching. Cole knew his brother hadn't been talking about the landscaping but about their relationship. Austin was very observant, and Cole hadn't been trying to hide anything anyway.

Cole grinned back at him. "She had dug up most of the old plants and relocated what she wanted to save before she ever let me come on board to help. Mom will love it."

"Yes, she will, and I like it too."

"Good. I like it because it makes the ranch look at one with its surroundings."

Austin laughed at that.

Tulip grinned at him. "Cole is getting in touch with his surroundings."

Austin studied them. "It's been good for both of you to just chill here, away from the tabloid mongers out there. How are you two doing emotionally? You especially, Tulip?"

"Better. After Harold called and said Darwin was completely done lying about what happened, I turned a corner. Playing in the ranch dirt has helped me heal, too."

Austin's expression was compassionate. "Good to hear. I'm glad Cole brought you here so you could have privacy during this time. Okay, I'm weary, and going to go in to see what Rose has fixed me to eat, and then I'm heading to bed. I have missed Rose's cooking."

They watched him go into the house and heard Rose exclaim hello and say she was glad that he was home as the door closed behind him.

Tulip smiled at Cole. "He's a good doctor. And a good man. I think Rose is filling in for your mom while she's gone. She loves you guys."

"Yes, she does. She's been with us since we were young. She's been with us through a lot, even went through us becoming these billionaires and all the craziness in our lives. She's family. And I can tell you, Austin really likes this. It's amazing. The other brothers are going to really like it, too. Levi came by yesterday and as you well know, he loved it."

"Yes, Levi reminds me of you in a lot of ways, except he's a little more jolly."

"Are you saying I'm too serious?" He wanted to kiss her again and show her he was not as serious as she thought; he was just trying really hard not to run her off.

"Maybe a little."

"We built this ranch from scratch and even though the cows have expensive oil wells scattered around and the ground underneath where they walk and eat is worth a lot of money, we want the ranch to still do well on its own. We were in the process of building a respectable ranch when we struck oil. I feel the weight of that dream still on my shoulders and work hard making sure the ranch is a separate entity from the oil wells and is profitable. I want to earn the respect of my peers the old-fashioned way—because I earned it, not because I struck oil. So, sometimes I neglect to let my walls down. And when I do, it seems I get set back, like this thing with Shelly. I've had it on my mind this week. I'm going to have to go see her, and I'm not looking forward to it." Not when he wanted to stay on the ranch and spend all his time with Tulip.

"I'm sorry you have to do that. But I believe you'll accomplish everything you set your mind to. Including working this out with Shelly. If she knows she's not telling the truth and that you aren't going to go back to her, then what does she have to gain, keeping up the charade?"

"Nothing but revenge, like Darwin tried to pile on you."

She placed a hand on his cheek, and his heart squeezed. "Cole, you just need to talk to her. I can understand why she would want you. I've never met a man like you. But no woman in her right mind would want a man who honestly had no feelings for her. Unless she's lost her mind. Or is terribly greedy. In that case, Harold can fix you up."

He placed a hand over hers and tugged her hand away from his face so he could place a kiss in her palm. She sucked in a breath and went very still. "Thank you for the pep talk. I think what I need right now is a break. And you deserve one more than anyone I know. So how about tomorrow, no work and I take you to the lake—you know, the one I told you about in the very beginning? The one you'll want to take a swim in."

She laughed. "I already told you I'm not swimming in any lake with no telling what might be swimming under my feet."

"Just humor me. Wear your swimsuit under your shorts and that way, if you want to go swimming, you'll be able to."

She took a deep breath, and then she nodded. "Okay, but I'm not guaranteeing anything. I'm highly opposed to it, just so you know."

He grinned. "I'm just glad you're going to wear your swimsuit under your shirt and shorts, so I'll have a shot at convincing you to take a chance."

She bit that lip he so much wanted to kiss. "All right, I guess I can do that."

Cole wanted to kick up his heels at her answer. Tomorrow couldn't get here soon enough.

CHAPTER THIRTEEN

"You were right. This is absolutely amazing." Tulip stood on the pier of a beautiful lake with near crystal-clear water because it was spring-fed. He'd explained it more to her on the way here, and now she understood why he had wanted her to come. Still, getting her into the water was another story. She was tempted, just because she wanted to go swimming with him.

He smiled at her from where he stood at the edge of the pier with his back to the water. "Yes, it is. I knew you'd love it."

He wore cargo shorts today and boat shoes and a bronze-toned T-shirt that stretched across his muscular torso and looked great with his amber eyes. He did not look like the stereotypical cowboy today.

"I like seeing you look relaxed, too. You've taught me today not to stereotype you cowboys. You look like you just got in from a fishing trip on the coast."

He gave her a smug look. "I like hearing that. You know, us cowboys do sometimes like to cool down at a lake and will even change out of jeans if it will help entice a beautiful woman into swimming. I'm giving it everything I've got to get you into that cool water with me. Contrary to worldwide belief, starched or even faded soft jeans do not do well in water. And although normally my brothers and I have been known to wear swim trunks instead of jeans—and there was a time where we didn't wear either—but because I'm in the presence of such a lovely lady, I've got my cargo shorts on, and underneath the cargo shorts I've got my swim trunks."

She laughed. "Don't tell me you're wearing a Speedo."

"That is stretching it for a cowboy. I said trunks. I've got on a pair of camouflage swim trunks almost as long as my cargo shorts. How about you? Are you ready to show me your swimsuit and I'll show you my swimsuit?"

She leaned against the railing of the pier with her hands behind her back. "Not so fast, cowboy. I haven't agreed to actually get into that water. I stuck my toe in a minute ago and it is cold."

He walked toward her, put a hand on either side of her and leaned in close. "Tulip Jones, you have worked me like a dog in that garden several days this week and it was hot. And you pretty much promised me you would get in that water. You have no idea how hard it has been for me to keep my hands off you. I've wanted to kiss you more than the couple of pecks that I have given you during the week that you have allowed to spontaneously happen. So, I'm just warning you that I'm going to keep you warm out there in that water."

Her pulse hummed at his words. She had had just as hard a week as he had. Ever since dinner with him, she had just wanted so much to be back in his arms. But they had both fought the attraction, except for the couple of sneaked kisses when it just seemed to fit.

She leaned in to accept the kiss she could sense he was about to give her. But now that they had got some of the hard work done and she had relaxed, she was going to be able to give him what he wanted in the beauty of this ranch yard that they had been working on. It was her way of paying him for all he had done for her since meeting him.

But now, could she let herself cross this line, into what she knew she wanted so badly? Her heart thundered in her ears as he leaned so close. All she had to do was move forward a little and they would be kissing.

"I don't know how any sane woman could say no to an amazing offer like that." Then she leaned forward and let their lips meet. She felt him smile against her lips and she smiled too, and then the kiss deepened.

He stepped forward and they were pressed together as his arms went around her and he held her close.

After a long enough time that her head was spinning and her feet felt as if they were no longer on solid ground, she cupped his face with her hands. "You, Cole Tanner, scare me."

He leaned his forehead against hers. "Don't be scared. That's one thing I don't ever want you to be about me, and that's scared."

Then he kissed her, briefly stepped back, and, with twinkling eyes, he unbuttoned his shorts and grinned at her. "If we're going in, it's swimsuit time…unless you want to go in like that."

"Fine, it's swimsuit time."

And with that, she tugged her shirt off over her head to reveal the red one-piece that she had bought that day he had taken her shopping, just in case she would get to use the beautiful pool at the house. She hadn't even ever thought she would be swimming in this gorgeous lake with this gorgeous man. He was not lying; he had on longer than knee-length camouflage swim trunks that hung on his hips. She nearly had a heart attack because of all that expanse of broad chest and muscle—yeah, the guy was just as stunning underneath his shirt as he was with his shirt on.

She had just hoped that she looked halfway decent in her swimsuit. She was one scrawny girl right now, although she had been eating, trying to put some curves on after having lost so much weight with worrying about the guy whose name she refused to mention any longer. "I'm thinking I need to eat more cinnamon rolls. I need some more curves."

A serious expression transformed his relaxed features as he took her hand. "Tulip, I think you probably lost a little more weight than you should have but I'll tell you one thing I have figured out this week knowing you, darlin', is that I'll take you any way you are. With fewer pounds or more pounds, I like you for you and that's all there is to it. And you are gorgeous."

Her heart melted. The guy knew what to say. "Your mama teach you to be such a sweet talker?"

"Hardly. I like to think I acquired that ability all on my own."

She decided just to grin at that one. Instead of answering him, she did something she never thought she would do—she playfully pushed him and he fell back toward the water.

She had just forgotten he was holding on to her hand and when he fell in, she went with him.

They hit the water and plunged into the chilly depths. When they came up, she was in his arms and he was laughing. And as she looked into his face and his warm eyes, she knew she would never feel for anyone what she felt for Cole.

She was in love with this amazing man.

* * *

He was falling for Tulip. He knew it was true, and he knew that Rose had spotted it before he had realized exactly how special he thought Tulip was. He had been a little bit slow on the uptake simply because of everything they had gone through in the first twenty-four hours of knowing each other. Their lives had been completely complicated and upended. The day she had been put in jail, he had watched her handle it with grace. And then, over the last week, being around her, watching her and getting to know her, he'd been drawn to her. He loved the quietness and the studious way she approached her work and the beauty of what she was seeing and creating. It all just came from inside her, as if the beauty inside her was escaping and beautifying everything she touched.

His mother's flower gardens were more beautiful than ever; she was very pleased when he'd sent her pictures. One day, he would get used to calling this his ranch, because this section belonged to him. His brothers were building up other sections and those were theirs, each of them putting in hard work and sweat and ingenuity. All of them determined that, together, they'd make the Tanner Ranches some of the best in Texas. And then well known around the United States.

Tulip was making its appearance live up to the vision, and his mother had said as much. He wanted her to meet Tulip. He wanted Tulip to meet his mother. Like Tulip and Rose got along, he knew she would get along with his mother. And as he sat on his horse, staring out across the land he loved while helping with a roundup, he knew why it was so important to him for his mother and Tulip to meet.

He had high hopes that maybe—just maybe—he had met the woman who could give him the happiness he wanted. That maybe Tulip was the woman who would help fulfill the destiny of this ranch. His parents had started this; they had loved so strongly and passionately and raised him and his brothers so diligently and compassionately here. They had had a great life growing up; they had worked hard from sunup to sundown, working the ranch—baling hay, planting oats, training horses, and herding and working cattle. They'd done it as a family together because they loved the land and ranching. They were building their legacies.

The oil hadn't changed that. Everyone else believed their lives had changed overnight. In many ways it had, but their love of the land and their dreams tied to the land had grounded them.

All the money did was complicate things in many ways. Oh, they had money to do with what they wanted, money to help with causes they felt strongly about, and they knew they were blessed. But it also caused them a bunch of headaches, like with the reporters and Shelly, which he hoped to get figured out in the coming week. He knew he wasn't the daddy to this baby Shelly might be carrying. He was relieved that Shelly would never be the mother to any of his children, but he knew he wanted children.

He wanted a family to raise here on this ranch. He wanted to be happy and love as beautifully and passionately as his parents had, and he wanted to raise some kids. He didn't know how many yet, but as he sat there on his horse, overlooking the ranch and cattle grazing with the river in the distance and the birds drifting around in the sky, his thoughts went to Tulip. She'd said she wanted children. His heart swelled thinking about the pretty, sweet babies she would make...the babies they would make. Together.

Would she even consider what he was thinking in his head and his heart?

Or was she just here, attracted to him, enjoying what they'd had the last few days since their trip to the lake?

He could not get that day out of his head. They had swam, cuddled in the water and kissed, and swam more and talked. She was funny and she was sweet, and she liked everything he had done with the ranch and what he thought about the ranch. She had said as much, but would she consider being a part of it? If she knew the direction his heart was going? Or would she look at the lifestyle that he had on the other side of that fence—the one where the cameras lurked and you never knew when they were going to put a story up that lied about them? And who knew what they might do if they were married and had children? Could she handle that?

Want to handle that?

"Hey, bro, you just going to sit there and daydream or you going to catch up with the herd?"

He looked over and saw Levi and his brother Jake riding up. "I guess I'll catch up. I was sitting here thinking about what a blessed group of guys we are to live on this land."

"I think that every day," Jake said, pulling up beside him. Jake had been on a trip to Montana to look at a large ranch they were thinking about buying in the cooler climate. They were always looking to expand and did a lot of business up north. "Montana is nice and big and has a lot of sky but this is home and I'm glad to be back."

"I agree with both of you, nothing prettier than hill country land." He frowned at Jake. "You're back just in time for the picture rats to be congregating at the gates and needling the heck out of Cole."

"Even before you called and warned me, I saw the tabloids. I came in the back way this morning. They drive me nuts and the last thing I want is to have them trailing me home in hopes I'll give them some dirt on Cole or Tulip. She sounds nice, from what Levi told me." He settled his steady gaze on Cole.

"She is real nice." Cole didn't feel like letting his feelings out just yet. What they could read on their own was all he could give right now as he figured things out for himself.

"He likes her more than he's letting on," Levi said, winking at him. "And as you can tell she's made the main ranch look like a million bucks. I'm thinking of trying to persuade her to come over and do some work for me?"

Jake laughed as he saw the warning glare Cole sent Levi.

"When she's done here you can try, but you better not be having any ideas about her." So much for not letting his feelings be known.

Levi grinned. "See Jake, I told you he likes her more than he was letting on. You were really sitting there thinking about Tulip, weren't you?"

Cole scowled at him.

"He told me you had it bad," Jake said. "I have to agree. Now I need to meet Tulip and see the woman whose got you all tied in love knots."

"That's a fact," Levi agreed. "And no worries big brother, Tulip wouldn't give me a second look. She's had eyes for you since the day you found her weaving down the road."

He gave up, needing their opinions for his sanity. "You think?"

Levi rested his wrist on his saddle horn and knocked his hat back a notch with his other hand as he squinted at Cole. "Yeah, I think it's true. But I know what you're worried about—same thing I'd be worried about—all that junk that goes on out past the gates. I hate it. I wished sometimes that we never struck that oil. Disrupts my life. It comes and goes, but right now I'm having to sneak in and out of my own ranch. So, yeah, Jake, keep them from knowing you're around as long as you can. I think they think they're going to get me to say something about your mess with Shelly Duncan. But I'm not going to say anything."

"Thanks, and I'm sorry you're having to deal with them."

Levi shrugged. "We've all brought it on us at different times. But anyway, right now the important thing is you have that beautiful woman working her little heart out on your yard. If you are serious about her—and I totally think you'd be a fool not to be then I wouldn't waste time. You can know things like that in less than a month. Might scare her off if she's not agreeable that people can fall in love in ten to fourteen days." He grinned.

"It's that serious?" Jake gaped at him.

"Yes, it is," Levi continued on a roll. "Me, personally, if I had a woman start telling me she was in love with me in ten to fourteen days, I'd probably run out of the building and never look back. So, I would proceed with caution. But I also would try not to let all this junk interfere in this relationship. Just let her see who you really are."

"Yeah," Jake agreed. "Just be real with her. This is pretty cool. I go away for a few days and come back to find my brother falling in love."

"I didn't say—" he started to say then stopped because he couldn't say it wasn't true.

Levi was right. So many things to consider. So many reasons for her to think he had lost his mind. Just that many more strikes against him. But then again, he had never been one who wasn't ready for a challenge.

"Maybe you need to stop worrying about what those tabloids are printing about you, kind of like I am, and start being yourself." Cole pressed the issue since Levi didn't mind handing him out advice. "Stop hiding in those dark corners at restaurants and eating alone. Go back to being the guy who enjoyed life, like you did before we struck oil."

"True, Levi, there is that," Jake said.

Levi pulled his hat back down over his eyes and nodded. "I hear what y'all are saying. We'll see. I figure it will hit me sooner or later, and I'll just blow all their minds with my antics—good, bad, or disappointing to them." Levi had been a partier before the tabloids had hounded him to death. Now he lay low and gave them nothing to print other than he was keeping a low profile. Jake had had his share too, but he was pretty good at avoiding them like today, coming in the back way.

"That's the only way to deal with them," he said.

"I guess so," Levi said. "By the way, Austin thinks you're falling for her too. He said so this morning before heading to the hospital."

"Are y'all taking bets or something?"

Jake laughed. "They are actually. But one thing you know, we're all rooting for you and your happiness."

"Thanks. That means a lot."

"True," Levi agreed. "Now, we better herd these cows so you can get home and stop daydreaming about Tulip and maybe get to sit on the swing with her."

"I'm all about that. Come on, you two, let's ride."

CHAPTER FOURTEEN

The reporters were gone. At last. But not before posting a picture that one of them had taken somehow of Cole kissing her. Her mother's phone call alerted her to the news.

"Tulip Michelle, do you know that you're on the front of the tabloid today kissing Cole?"

Tulip gasped, "How, Mama? We haven't been anywhere."

"Well, darling, you might not have been anywhere, but this picture clearly shows you and that gorgeous Cole Tanner kissing among some pretty flowers and rosebushes. Everyone in the shop was in a hullabaloo talking about it this morning. I hadn't even gotten to the shop and Beulah Anne had already about had a heart attack running across the street to show me the front cover of the tabloid she'd bought at the Piggly Wiggly. There were others after her waving copies of the same magazine. They want you and Cole to do an autograph signing."

"Tell them no, Mama. This is awful." She realized the picture had to be of when he'd kissed her among the roses in the front yard. She hung her head for a minute, so sick of the photographers and of the turmoil they'd caused in her life since she'd run away from her wedding. "And for the record, the photo is real," she said, unable to keep the exasperation out of her voice. "Cole kissed me in the front yard. Someone must have been standing on the roof of a van or something to get the shot from the front gate. I hate this."

"Awe, honey, I'm sorry. But I think Cole is a really nice person and everyone at the salon is going to be thrilled for you. But are you sure you can handle this kind of attention? Is he worth being on the front of these tabloids? Because I have a feeling, this won't be the last time."

Tulip rubbed her forehead, feeling a dull throb of

worry. This was something she had anticipated always being a problem for him. But until recently she hadn't thought it might always be her problem too. Not until recently, as her feelings had shifted into longing for a deeper relationship with Cole. But now, thinking forward and being truthful with herself about the possibility of them becoming a couple and maybe even a married couple. She knew it was too much.

She didn't want to always hide behind walls and bushes trying to stay out of the limelight. This morning's news had sideswiped her with a reality check.

"I'll have to get back to you on that one, but I guess just try to keep the rumors down. We're simply two normal people who happen to like each other. He's a cowboy who wants to be a regular person and things like this are just something that happens."

"I understand that but right now the tabloid headline is not good."

She cringed. "And it would say what?"

"Runaway bride homewrecker of Good Morning Hill Country's Shelly Duncan and her billionaire cowboy, Cole Tanner. Baby on the way left fatherless."

And that was too much. Tulip's mouth fell open as she yanked the phone away from her ear and stared at the screen as if anybody other than herself could see her dismayed expression. Closing her eyes, she sucked in a breath and counted to three, trying to calm her erratic heartbeat.

She put the phone back up to her ear. "Mama, I need to go right now. That is all a bald-faced lie, and it is ridiculous, and I have just about had it."

"Now, honey, calm down. Don't go out there and make a fool of yourself any more than this is trying to goad you into doing right now. Just like you and Cole told me not to take my shotgun on my front porch, don't you go doing it either with a real shotgun or your loaded mouth. Take a few more deep breaths, calm down and go tell Cole about these headlines. Far as I'm concerned, it's that young man's time to get this handled. If that baby is not his then surely with all that money he's got and that high-powered Harold lawyer dude, he can fix this situation."

"Yes, that's what I'm thinking too, but I'm sure he's about to be as startled by this as I am. Alright, love you Mom, bye."

With that she hung up and then dropped her hoe, so that she didn't head straight for the gates to use it as a weapon, then she stormed toward the house. She thought Cole might be in his office as usual first thing in the mornings. At least she hoped he was. This had to stop.

She was not a homewrecker.

True, she had been a runaway bride. But she had not stolen anything from Shelly Duncan and she certainly had not made a baby fatherless.

* * *

"Harold, I have stayed away from Shelly and not confronted her, but Levi just snapped a shot of this morning's tabloid and texted it to me. It's not good. I'm warning you I'm going to see Shelly myself unless you get her to retract all these statements she's making. I've got to do something."

"Cole, we are working on it. You have to be patient."

"No, I don't."

He listened to Harold tell him all the reasons why he needed to stay put.

"Harold, they're spreading more rumors about Tulip, and yes, I'm very interested in Tulip, and yes, I kissed Tulip in the front yard."

"Didn't you think about the tabloids and their tripods on top of their vans?"

"When I did it, I realized afterwards that if a cameraman was on top of a van with a tripod, he might get a shot. But at the moment, I was not thinking about intrusive photographers. I was thinking about other things." He'd been only thinking about feeling Tulip in his arms kissing him. "I should have warned Tulip about it, but this is going to blindside her if she hasn't already heard about it." Cole paced the room and raked both hands through his hair.

"I will call her right now. And tell her we are suing her for slander. She's ignoring us right now and says she'll only deal with you, but there's no reason for you to go deal with her. If you show up there, you're going to have your picture snapped some more and there's no telling what they'll start writing. My hope is she'll just back off. We can offer her money—"

"No. Do not offer her money. I am not about to go through life being blackmailed by people who are trying to spread lies about me. I refuse to do that."

He hated this. And he hated it most because poor Tulip was going to be slandered even more. It was ridiculous. He felt like he was using her, just like Darwin had. He knew it wasn't true, but still, he could have come clean that day he kissed her in the garden. Should have told her what to expect, and he'd hoped that maybe their kiss hadn't been intruded on by the trash out there snapping shots for money.

"Harold, I'm giving you an hour, two hours at the most and I'm getting in my truck and I'm going that way—" His door slammed open and a very pale, very angry looking Tulip stood glaring at him. "Harold, deal with it. I've got more important business right now." He clicked the button off.

He knew she knew by the dazed look on her face.

"Tulip, I know what you've seen. I just saw it too, and that's why I was on the phone with Harold."

"I don't want to be rude but obviously Harold's not getting the job done. I'm not a homewrecker. I am not taking a baby's daddy away."

He walked over to her and took her by the shoulders, wanting so badly to take her into his arms. "I know that it's all lies, and it's breaking my heart that it's out there like that. I've not gone to see Shelly because Harold told me not to. He's my lawyer, and he's been recommending I hold back hoping that it would just blow over and she would admit with the pressure he's putting on her that she's just been trying to get at me or has made a mistake. He's trying to give her a way out. But I just told him If he can't get her to agree to retract some of this stuff in two hours then I'm going to see her."

"And that might make it worse?"

"Yeah, it could. It will mean probably that many more photos will be taken. I'm pretty sure that there are paparazzi up there hanging out with her right now because she's fueling the fire with this mini press ops she's holding. But this picture they took, that's my fault. I should have never kissed you in the front yard."

He squeezed her shoulders and then let go and rubbed his temple. "I just wasn't thinking. It's not your fault, whatever you think, none of this is your fault. I, on the other hand, knew that sometimes photos could be snapped from that position, but I wanted to kiss you so much that day I lost my head and did it. And not one moment, not one ounce of my heart has regretted that kiss until now. I hate that you had such a lie spread about you in the tabloid. Especially after going through the days with Darwin's lies."

She took a deep breath and looked like she was a little steadier as she walked around him and strode to the window, placed her hand on the window frame and stared at the gardens. He walked up behind her wanting to touch her, wanting to hold her but deciding against it and instead walked over to the fireplace. Putting distance between them because he didn't blame her if she never wanted him to touch her again. He waited, giving her a chance to calm down.

After a minute, she turned toward him; some of the color had come back into her face now, and for that he was thankful. Her beautiful green eyes were sad. "I don't know if I can do this."

The words he had dreaded hearing her say, the words he'd expected ever since Levi texted him the cover of the tabloid. They hadn't talked about a future, but he had been ready to.

"I understand. I know that this is more than most people can deal with and I get that. I was a fool when I asked Shelly out. I don't know what I was thinking that day. I guess I had just pulled back so far from the spotlight and from worrying about dating someone for this very reason, and when I met Shelly at that charity drive, she seemed genuine. Levi didn't trust her from the beginning and within two dates, I knew he was right. You can't hide your true self for very long if the person you're hiding it from is the least bit leery. And I have paid for the fact that on that second date I didn't end it right then. I kept thinking maybe I was wrong, so I carried it on for almost a month and I have not been able to live it down. And I brought you into it."

"And there's where you're wrong, Cole. You didn't bring me into this. I brought you into this when I ran away from Darwin and wrecked my car and you saved me. I'll never forget that. So, don't blame yourself. Despite what's going on right now, I never ever will regret knowing you. But I don't think I can continue to do this. Just the bit of limelight Darwin got with his business and the times he was in the spotlight didn't help me feel comfortable with marrying him among a lot of other reasons that led to me running away. But since running away and crashing the car and him and his untruths…it has been so much more escalated. And then knowing that you may always have the potential to draw the media to you, I can't let myself fall for you. This is not the kind of life I'm looking for."

Him either. "I get it." He hated it but he did get it. "I wouldn't want you to have to go through this all the time either." His insides were sick. "If you want to leave today, I'll pay for what you've done, and we'll call it a deal. The place looks great."

They stared at each other, his heart was breaking

but she didn't know he had crossed the line a long time ago and fallen for her. She didn't know that he had hoped to ask her to marry him and she wouldn't know. There was no sense in adding that to her plate of worry. And he didn't want her to feel like she owed him anything. He couldn't in any way guilt her into it or anything that remotely resembled anything what Darwin or the other guy, Joe, had done to her.

"If it's okay with you, I think I'll finish out what I'm doing with that one flower bed and then it's pretty much done. You could hire someone to come in and add a few more plants to the look or I can send you my layout and suggestions and you could plant them. But I think I'll leave tonight. I still have a week on my vacation time, so who knows I might just sneak into my condo and pack a bag then get out of town. I might go find me a nice quiet cabin somewhere far away from all these paparazzi and chill for a week. Maybe once you let them know I'm no longer here and that our budding relationship ended, maybe they'll leave you alone too. And when I come back to town everything will be better."

He hated to say it, but for her that might work. "I think that's a great idea. I will deposit the money." She'd already given him her information for an earlier deposit he'd insisted on for the initial payment. "Any idea where you're going to go?"

"Probably not here in the Hill Country. Maybe I'll go up north past Dallas."

"That's a good long drive."

"Did I ever tell you that I like road trips? I do, I am a road trip kind of girl. The problem's just going to be getting far enough away from folks who don't care about the Hill Country nor what's going on with the sweetheart of the Hill Country. And as far as I can tell, we aren't important enough to be on the national news so it should all be good."

"Thank goodness, at least we have that going for us. Look, I'll take you to your condo later tonight, may need to wait until after dark. I'll meet you at the old truck behind the barn at say, nine-thirty, is that good?"

That was right; she didn't have a way to get past the front gate or get home. "Yes. I'll be ready." She turned to go, then went to him. She raised up on her tiptoes and kissed him gently on the lips.

Cole couldn't help it he hugged her close, wrapped his arms around her and just held her and buried his face in her hair and just took a moment to breathe her in and catalogue it to his memory bank. "You take care of yourself, Tulip Jones, and if you ever need anything you know where to find me."

Her voice was thick as his. "I know. You take care of yourself." And then she pulled out of his arms, strode across the room and walked out of his life.

* * *

Rose was off today. She wouldn't be able to tell the sweet lady good-bye. She'd send her a card, but it wasn't the same.

It was just one of many thoughts that hurt as Tulip slipped out the kitchen door and back into the sunshine. Her eyes burned with tears that she fought not to unleash. Cole had been so understanding, and he'd let her go without even a slight fight. Her heart ached with that knowledge.

She had been working on an area around a

waterfall that she'd created in one of the large flower beds in the circular drive. It had been an added inspiration after having gotten in her load of rocks. She loved waterfalls, and this one simulated a running brook that flowed from between two larger rocks, down to mid-sized and then smaller, and then a curving rocky brook among lantana and sage and a few other plantings. Now she finished setting the last of the sunny yellow lantana. Then she walked around the grounds, checking on all that she'd accomplished in the two weeks that she'd been here, hiding out from the world. A world that had not left her alone but hounded her and lied about her.

She saw Cole back his truck out of the garage and head down the drive toward the front entrance. Sadness and anger boiled inside her at the idea of being used, not by him but by Darwin, and Shelly and the reporters. She wanted to march down that drive and tell them to all get a life and leave hers alone. But she wouldn't. It would only make it worse.

Despite their teasing about Cole teaching her how to say no, they'd never actually gotten around to any classes on the subject. But she'd learned it anyway. She'd also learned that sometimes even when you were straightforward with your intentions, like Cole had been with Shelly, things could still be used against a person if the person wanted to hurt the other.

Sighing, her shoulders slumped, she headed toward the cabin. Both she and Cole had both gone out with dates who were selfish and untruthful, and they'd both been bitten.

When she got back to the cabin, she showered and changed clothes and then packed a colorful duffel bag full of the small supply of clothing and toiletries she purchased that first day after arriving at the ranch. She didn't feel like eating anything but took a glass of tea to the porch swing and waited for nine-thirty. She knew when it came time, she would pick up her bag and walk to the back side of the barn where Cole kept his beat-up ranch truck. He or Levi would be waiting. And then, just like that first day—because no one could see this truck as it headed through the pasture to the gravel road—they would take his secret escape from his own property.

CHAPTER FIFTEEN

Cole walked down the paved path that wound along the Comal River in San Marcos. After Tulip had come to his office in so much pain, it hurt his heart more desperately than he'd ever believed possible. He'd been determined to fix this somehow, and that meant going against his lawyer's advice and calling a meeting with Shelly.

Her studio was here in downtown San Marcos, but no way was he going there. He'd called a public meeting here, in the busy park overlooking the people and tube-filled blue waters of the winding river that thousands flocked to in warm weather. It was a busy place, and he hoped Shelly would honor her promise of coming alone. They weren't important enough for this chaos surrounding them. There had still been four cars waiting across the road from his ranch. Thankfully, the traffic in San Marcos was bad enough near the highway that he'd been able to lose them. But if she brought them with her, he was stuck. He was willing to try it, if it meant getting her to tell the truth and help Tulip.

He leaned against a tree where he could watch for her and soon he spotted her walking down the path in her high heels and soft pink suit. With her blonde hair and blue eyes and the way she carried herself, she always drew attention. Here, in an expensive body-hugging suit when everyone else wore swimsuits and sported inner tubes and snorkels, she stood out. But he'd chosen this spot on the off chance that most of these people were from out of town or other parts of Texas and didn't watch her popular morning show viewed by Hill Country locals.

Thankfully, no one approached her for an autograph. And it didn't appear that she was being trailed by reporters. He moved onto the path and she spotted him. He, too, stood out in his Stetson and jeans—not exactly the attire someone would wear here on a hot day.

"Cole."

She said his name with what he assumed was supposed to be a sexy drawl. He did not find it appealing.

"I'm glad you agreed to meet me."

She smiled, and her gaze raked slowly down him. "I was glad you finally called. We have so much to talk about. And that awful lawyer of yours doesn't seem to understand that this was something we had to discuss privately." She walked closer, then looked around. "I just wish you hadn't suggested here. It's hot and so crowded."

"I didn't want any of your media friends around. We need to talk about this lie you're telling about me and your baby. You know I'm not the father. We don't know each other well enough for me to be the father." They'd had a few goodnight kisses, and that had been it.

She frowned. "Only you know that. I'm just telling them that so you would start seeing me again."

"Why?" He really had started to believe the woman was delusional. "We are looking for different things out of life. You know this is wrong and you need to tell the truth now. This isn't just about you trying to use me anymore."

Her eyes flashed. "Don't tell me what I need to do. I believe we make a great team. You haven't given us a fair chance. And then this Tulip, the runaway bride, came along and took all your time and snagged the headlines. I needed something to get your attention and what better ploy than a baby?"

"But it's a lie. How are you going to continue this? What purpose does it serve?"

She moved close to him and before he could step back, she placed her hand on his chest and leaned toward him. "It serves my purpose. My ratings are down, and when I was dating you, my ratings skyrocketed and made my employers very happy." She suddenly looked desperate. "I need you, Cole. And the baby helped ratings too." Her gaze shifted from him and then back as she took another step closer. The tree that Cole had stupidly put behind him rather than next to him trapped him for just long enough for Shelly to press her body against him and raise her face to his.

He looked down at her, startled, and slid sideways, leaving her staring at him. "Shelly, I'm sorry about your trouble but this is not helping matters between us. I have no idea what you thought it would accomplish."

He had a really bad feeling now, knowing full well that her rubbing against him had been a photo op and he'd fallen for it. He could already see the tabloids. Suddenly he knew there was more to this entire story. "Are you paying these bozos? Is that why they are persisting in hanging around my entrance when I'm not usually newsworthy enough to hold them for more than a night or two?" He didn't have to hear her deny or admit it; he knew it was true.

She smiled coyly, and he felt like throwing up on her expensive high heels. Boy, that would make a splendid picture, he thought and then felt bad about it.

"Cole, think about what a great team we would make. You and your money and me and my contacts—we could be the power couple of the area. Think of the charities we could help, and the romantic story of how we met while helping with the charity to save wild horses. I know you aren't a big dater. You told me so on our first date. And how the money is sometimes a noose around your neck."

Why had he admitted something that personal to Shelly? Sometimes he wondered about himself. He sighed and held his ground rather than storming off and letting his temper get the better of him.

She added, "As a unit, I could take the limelight and let you do your thing…ranch or whatever."

A unit? "Shelly, I'm not wanting to be part of a unit. Look, we have nothing in common. And so there was no reason to continue to date. I just wanted to part ways and continue as friends. But now, with this lie you're pushing, I'm done. You need to stop this charade. My lawyers are not kidding. I'm not going to just let you go around telling people I'm a man who would run out on his baby. If you're carrying a baby, we both know it's not mine. And I'll demand a paternity test. Sycamore has told you that already." It wasn't a question because he knew Harold had told her. "These tabloids are hurting more than just you and me."

Her expression hardened and there was nothing pretty about her as her eyes flashed. "You're talking about Tulip Jones. What kind of name is that, anyway? She came into the picture and messed everything up. How do you think I felt when I saw you kissing her?" She flung the words at him.

He narrowed his gaze and realized a few people had heard her outburst. He needed to keep this calm. He'd never experienced anything like this from a woman. "Shelly, we were finished before Tulip showed up."

Her face hardened, and her eyes could have cut through steel. "No, you're wrong. I was winning you back."

This was getting out of hand. He rubbed his eyebrow, feeling a headache coming on. Letting out a long breath to get his temper under control, he tested the waters. "You weren't winning me back. But this, right now, isn't helping you, me, or Tulip. What do you expect me to do, marry you? I'm further away now from liking you as a person than I was prior to this meeting."

"Just give me another chance. I can make it good for you. I promise." She stepped close again and ran a long nail along his arm before he pulled back.

"No, not happening. I see this is getting nowhere. Expect my lawyer to contact you, and I will be suing." Not waiting around for any more tricks, he turned and headed back toward the exit and his truck. He knew he'd been had and could already see the headlines and the photos. He pulled his hat low to at least shadow his face as he wasn't sure which direction the cameras were located; he only knew they were there.

And that he hadn't done anything to help Tulip. Or their relationship.

More than likely, just as Harold had warned, the photos and headlines in the tabloids tomorrow would do away with any hope he ever had of getting her back.

* * *

It was Levi waiting on her in the truck. Disappointment descended on her like a night without stars and no moon.

"Thanks for giving me a ride," she said to Levi as he pushed away from where he'd been leaning against the tailgate waiting for her.

His handsome face was marred by the concerned frown. "Let me take that for you." He took her bag and placed it in the back of the truck. "I'm sad to see you go." He paused as if he was going to say more but instead, he reached for the passenger side door handle and opened the door for her. "Hop in and we'll blow this joint." He gave her a wiry smile.

He was special and she appreciated him not giving her a hard time about leaving. "Thanks. I hate to go."

His amber eyes, so like Cole's flickered but all he did was nod and then closed the door for her after she'd slid onto the seat and reached for her seatbelt. She clasped her hands together after snapping her seatbelt on as he strode around and then slid into the driver's seat.

She didn't say anything as Levi drove across the pasture without lights and entered the trees where the road cut through to the other pastures and then to the gate that was overgrown and semi-hidden. Levi got out of the truck and strode to the large tangle of bushes that looked as if they were overgrown and the gate was unused. Reaching down, he grabbed the old rope that hung out at the edge and he pulled the lightweight bundle of bushes that were intertwined together out of the way. Tulip had watched Cole do this her first day here, and they went shopping and she'd thought then how sad it was they had to go through this much to have privacy. Now, watching Levi, her heart ached with how wrong this was. Once the bush bundle on this side of the fence was pulled out of the way, he opened the old gate, then picked up one bundle of dried bushes and tossed it to the side, then did the same for the other bush. He returned to the truck and drove them through the gate, then stopped the truck and closed the gate. She noticed he didn't put the bushes back. It was dark and he'd be back in a couple of hours. Cole had replaced everything the day they'd gone shopping, but it had been daylight.

To Tulip, it was sad either way.

They'd driven by her own place saw two different cars with a person just sitting inside…waiting. She'd called her mother, and she'd said there was no unfamiliar or paparazzi cars she recognized on her street at the moment. So, to her mother's house they went.

They'd spoken a little but had been avoiding important conversation. Now, as Levi pulled to a halt at the curb, the tension between them magnified.

"Levi, thank you for everything you did for me."

He nodded, his eyes glinting in the dashboard lights. "It was my pleasure."

She pushed the door open and to her surprise he got out too. He walked around and pulled her bag from the back of the truck. "I'll carry this for you."

"You don't have to." She didn't need her mother pulling him into the house and prolonging this parting. She needed every bit of her ties with Cole behind her or she might crumble. And besides that, she knew that Levi had more to say, and she was afraid to hear what it was he was holding back. She took a firm grip of the bag and when Levi didn't let go, she sighed. "Levi, what it is you want to say?"

He sighed too and let go of the bag. "It's just, in

this crazy short time you've been in my brother's life he's been happier than I've ever seen him. Even with all the idiots hounding y'all. When he looks at you it's clear, he cares for you. And I'm going to go way out on a limb and say he loves you. So, for what it's worth coming from me, I wish you'd give him a second chance. Life is not always like this. The money shot takers and users are just stirred up because of the lies Shelly Duncan's been spreading. That's going to fade. And if Cole says that baby isn't his, then it isn't. My brother is one of the good guys. I just want you to remember that. And he deserves happiness too. For some reason he's not telling you that, so I wanted to do it for him."

Her insides knotted up on top of feeling as if she was standing on the deck of a ship in a ferocious storm. "Thank you, Levi. And I know he's one of the good guys. This isn't about that. It's about all the lies swirling around because of Shelly. And though hers will go away, there is always potential for new stories. I just can't do it."

She had the urge to kiss Levi's cheek but just in

case there were cameras around she didn't do it. That also was wrong, always being afraid to act on feelings of her heart. Instead, she walked away but turned a few steps down the sidewalk to look back at him. He had just started toward his truck door with a grim expression on his face.

"Levi," she said, and he paused. "You're one of the good guys too."

He nodded, tipped his hat and got in his truck.

She went to the house, and they went their separate ways.

CHAPTER SIXTEEN

It had been seven days, three hours, and twenty-four minutes since she'd last seen Cole Tanner. She could probably count the seconds, but that would really be obsessing, and she'd been trying not to. After Levi had driven her to her mother's house late that last night at Cole's, she'd taken her mother's Malibu and driven to a cabin on Lake Palestine. Not the other side of Dallas, but still more central Texas, heading toward Louisiana. Oh, they still had the tabloids, but she'd called in her grocery order at a store with curbside delivery and had the cabin owner leave the key under the mat. No one had been close enough to care or see who was moving into the cabin on the lake. She'd worn a floppy hat and laid out by the water's edge and tried all week to relax.

And to not think about Cole.

That had been hard to do. Even before her mother called and told her that Cole had been on the front cover of a tabloid, kissing Shelly Duncan. The headline had stated that they were back together, and the homewrecker had moved out of Cole's home.

She'd never lived in his home, though she'd stayed there that first night, but that was not the kind of living in his home the tabs were implying.

She pinched the bridge of her nose to keep the tears from flowing. She'd known in her heart that this was just another lie. But even so, he'd gone to see her and somehow they'd kissed. Her mother had taken a picture of the front page and sent it to her. It had been jarring to see them so close. His hat had been bent over her, obscuring the kiss—but it looked like a kiss. Looked like what a picture of him and her kissing would have looked like if the camera had been on the other side of his hat. It just so happened that the photo of Tulip and Cole kissing had been with the camera on the side, exposing their lips locked together.

That had been the first day at the lake. The second

day, her mother had sent another photo. This one was of them standing close, wearing the same clothes, but Shelly had been smiling flirtatiously and running a fingernail along his arm. Cole had not been moving away. The headline that day was the lovebirds were moving in together and picking out baby furniture. There were a lot of other photos, her mother said, photos she and all her lady clients believed were old photos photoshopped in front of baby stores.

As much as she hated looking, she had stared at those photos for the longest time. She knew full well that he was not moving in with Shelly. And yet, this was what he had to live with.

Why was this happening?

It just didn't make sense.

And yet, she knew she didn't want to deal with being on the front cover of a tabloid again. She tried to imagine if this was her and Cole married and expecting their own baby, and they were having to see their photos splashed on the tabloids. She hated it.

She knew Cole did, too, and her heart went out to him. She just wanted to give him a hug.

Three days went by and suddenly there were no photos on the cover of the tabloids. And her mother had called and told her that everyone had read every tabloid out there and that no photos or write-ups were in them.

Her heart hoped that maybe this was the end of it.

And then, yesterday, the tabloids were lit up with the headlines that Shelly had never been pregnant. It had just been a ploy to keep Cole. Oh, what a big day the tabloids had at Shelly's expense.

Tulip's heart had skipped with happiness.

Harold had come through for Cole. Or Cole had come through somehow.

For now, it seemed he was free from the stories. But she knew there would just be more later on. He would have to live with this intrusion into his private life—always.

And she just couldn't do it.

Could she?

Feeling horrible, she had packed up her mother's car and headed home. She suspected that she was yesterday's news. At least, she hoped so. What she knew for a fact was it was time to rebuild her business, if she could. Cole had compensated her extremely well; she didn't have to rush, but she needed to get busy. An idle mind did not work for her. It gave her no peace from the thoughts of Cole and what could have been if only he hadn't been a billionaire the tabloids loved.

She didn't take her mother's car home immediately. Instead, she went to her condo and was relieved there were no strange vans hanging around. Or men in her flower beds. She called her mom and told her she'd come home a day early and would bring the car the next day.

After locking her door behind her, she showered and then pulled out a container of strawberry ice cream that she'd bought just before the day of her wedding that never happened. She was eating it on the back patio, wishing for the porch swing of her little cabin at Cole's, when her mother called and told her to watch the evening news rerun on her computer.

"Why, Mama?"

"Tulip, honey, I love you, but if you don't turn on

that computer right this minute, I am going to scream or come over there and put you in time-out."

Startled by her mother's serious tone, she quickly agreed. "Okay, Mama, I'll do that right now. I promise."

"Good." She hung up.

That was strange. She walked to her office and turned on her computer. Then she sank into the chair and tapped in the news station and found the replay of the evening news.

She didn't have to wait long before seeing the reason her mother had been so adamant that she watch the news. Cole, so handsome—so haggard-looking—stood at his entrance gates and faced the reporters.

"I'm making one last statement and then I'm going to take the advice of a nice little lady I met not too long ago, and I'm going to start using my shotgun full of buckshot on trespassers—that includes on this entrance and the one across the street, since I just bought that property too. And I'll be aiming at you. I've put up with the lies of Shelly Duncan, who I just learned is no longer at the morning show. I could never have been the father of a child of hers and because of you intruding on my privacy, I've lost the love of my life. Yeah, you heard me right. I love Tulip Jones. And you've done what you set out to do—you've helped destroy that. So there, be happy and get off my land. You won't have to worry about me giving you any more news. I'm done, stick a fork in me."

And then he'd pushed a button, and the gates closed; he walked away and down the long drive away from the reporters. The camera followed him in the distance as the broadcaster wrapped up the segment.

Tulip didn't hear a word he said; she just watched Cole walking down the lane to his ranch. He'd said he loved her. He'd said it to a camera, letting them into his head—a place she knew he did not ever let them into. But he'd looked so sad. So alone.

And he'd said he loved her.

She swallowed the hard lump in her throat. Every instinct in her told her to go to him. To tell him she loved him too. But he hadn't said anything about wanting her. He'd just told them he loved her and it was over.

Her head swam as she thought of Joe kneeling down in that stadium and asking her to marry him. She'd felt so sorry for him and accepted his proposal. And she'd run away. And then Darwin, and how he'd used her to get her to marry him so his mother would see him married before she died. And then he'd turned out to be a liar and a jerk who would even use his mother! Harold had contacted her with information, at Cole's request, so that she wouldn't fret any more about running away from Darwin. Cole's investigator had learned that the only thing Darwin's mother was being treated for by a doctor was for an ingrown toenail.

A toenail.

She really knew how to pick them.

Except, she knew without a doubt that Cole wasn't like Darwin or Joe.

He had been the real deal. A keeper.

And she loved him so much. With all of her heart, she'd loved him. Still loved him.

It was just the attention from the media that she couldn't handle.

He knew this and hadn't asked her to stay for him. He hadn't told her he loved her. He'd told them. The big gesture like what Darwin and Joe had done? Was it to try and get her back?

No. It wasn't the same and she knew this.

Her heart hurt. It hurt so deep that it ached and cracked, and she couldn't move.

* * *

Cole sat on his porch, angry at himself for storming down the gate and letting the reporters see how much they'd gotten to him. He'd told them he loved Tulip.

Why had he done that? Public declarations were the last thing she would want from him. If by some chance she saw his outburst and declaration, she'd be upset, because it would be another form of manipulation of her feelings. He didn't want her thinking he was trying to guilt her into coming back to him.

But he did want her back. After he'd gone through last week, getting Shelly to admit that he wasn't the daddy to her baby, it had been a very bad week. He didn't like forcing someone to be honest, but Jensen had dug up proof that she'd lied about a baby once before to coerce a man into marrying her. Once Harold had given the information to someone he used to leak information he wanted to get out when he wanted it to, the story had come out.

She'd lost her job and in the end she'd admitted he wasn't the dad, and there was no baby in the first place. Cole felt bad that she'd lost her job, but she'd already told him her ratings were down and this was a stunt to try and keep it. His brothers and Harold had reminded him that he wasn't the one who lied. He'd just made the mistake of dating her and then going and confronting her, giving the tabloids more fuel.

Which he'd done again tonight. No, tonight he hadn't given them more fuel, he'd lost it tonight and exploded everything.

His phone rang. It was Levi but when he picked up, it was a conference call from Bret and Levi both calling him from a local sports bar where they'd been eating.

"You're completely messed up in the head, Cole." Levi shook his head on the screen. "Bret and I just watched you on TV. You're all over the local news."

Bret took the phone. "Hey, I just got to town and am trying to eat my supper when I look up at the TV blasting out clips of you declaring your love for Tulip. You look like a deranged hermit storming back into the darkness like a Sasquatch. I need to meet this girl who has you all tied in knots. She must be something and from what Levi says, she is worth losing your mind over."

He'd really lost his mind. "Yeah, she's worth it. But all of this is simply too much for her and I get it. I can't even deal with it."

"From a guy who lives in the limelight because I choose to, being on the pro bull riding circuit, it is a lot to handle. I'm hoping you two can figure things out."

"Not happening. I can't ask her to deal with it."

The sound of honking coming from the front gates had him standing up. What was going on? "Hey fellas, I need to go. Talk to you later."

He clicked the app on his phone and his video

monitors came up. He tapped the front gate and went still at what he saw. Tulip stood beside her car as she honked her horn and glared up at the video camera she knew was trained on her. When a reporter—yes, they were still hanging around—asked a question; she poked a finger in his chest and told him to back off. He did exactly that and Cole laughed, watching the startled expression on the man's face.

What was she up to?

He hopped off the porch, jogged to his ATV, and slid behind the wheel. He could have walked back down there but it wasn't a short walk and he wanted to see Tulip now. The ATV was fast and had him there within seconds.

When she saw him approaching, she stopped honking and waited for him to push the button. She glared at the reporters. "You want a story? Well, start taping because I'm about to give you your wish—so don't miss it." And then she walked toward him. The lights of the ATV illuminated her as she came to stand in front of him.

"What are you doing?" Cole asked, loving every

line and curve of her face as she stared at him with earnest eyes. He wanted to hold her. To never let her go. But that wasn't his call.

"I'm doing what I should have done before. I'm doing this my way."

And then, to his complete surprise, she went down on one knee right there in front of him and the cameramen and whoever would be watching this when it went live.

"I love you, Cole Tanner, and I don't care who knows it. I don't care if I have to point my finger at the cameramen for the rest of my life and tell them to butt out of my business every day for the rest of my life. Because if that's what I need to do, I'll do it, as long as I get to spend the rest of my life with you by my side. The one thing I've learned this week is I can't control what they write. I can't control if they spread lies and I can't control if people out there want to believe what they say. But I can control my own future happiness, and that means I have to have you in my life. So, right here, and right now, without care of who is watching this—and with the full knowledge that you could turn me down—I'm asking you to marry me, if what you said earlier is true. Because I love you, Cole. I love you with every breath in my body, now and forever. But I'm not looking for sympathy. I'm fully aware that you know how to say no and I'm glad of it. Because I'm looking for forever, so please say no if you're not looking for the same thing."

He could not believe his ears or his eyes. She was throwing the big gesture at him with the cameras rolling and pictures flashing. And he loved it.

And he loved her with all of his heart.

Reaching down, he cupped her shoulders with his hands and, if she could do it so could he so right there for the world to see, he went down on one knee in front of her.

"Tulip Jones, I've loved you almost from the moment I met you, and I will take you as my wife any way I can get you. Even if it's with a camera strapped to your head. But I promise you, I'll do whatever it takes to get rid of these jokers. But right now, all I want is you, forever in my life. Will you marry me?"

She smiled brilliantly. Dazzling him and the

flashing cameras as she threw her arms around his neck. She held him tightly, then planted a kiss on his lips as if tomorrow were never coming.

Cole wrapped his arms around her, hugged her, molding her to him and enjoyed the ride.

He adored her, needed her, loved her with all of his heart and planned to make certain she never wanted to let him go. He knew that with her by his side, he could face anything that came their way.

EPILOGUE

Levi Tanner watched his brother Cole dancing with his soulmate, Tulip. The wedding had been attended by a large number of friends and family here at the main ranch, among the beautiful landscaping that Tulip had done. Levi stood near the outer edge of the dance floor, observing, like he liked to do. And at the table on the other side of the huge turquoise ceramic pot of flowers was the table where Tulip's mother and some of her friends were sitting and enjoying themselves.

"That Tulip Michelle is just the most beautiful bride I have ever seen, Mira."

"Why, thank you, Beulah Anne. I was thinking the very same thing. If any of those horrible tabloid people are here, she will take all their readers' breath away in that dress. And my new son-in-law isn't shabby himself. Those Tanner men do have the looks, don't they?"

"You are right about that. You are going to have some gorgeous grandbabies." Beulah Anne cocked her blue-haired head and met Levi's gaze that had momentarily drifted to the ladies' table. She smiled. "That Levi is a showstopper, that one." She winked at him; he tipped his head and then immediately put his gaze somewhere else.

Tabloids. The mere mention of the creepy reporters who liked to stalk them had him surveying the wedding goers. They'd backed off Tulip and Cole after the flashy show Tulip had put on for them that night she'd said to heck with them and proposed to Cole at the gate, in full view of God and everyone. The videos had trended online as the Runaway Bride Gets Her Man and she had succeeded in turning the tide on the bad news that Shelly had tried to bury them under. Tulip's business had flourished after the proposal went viral. And, all in all, the world was all rosy for them, though she swore that soon they would be able to settle down and have a normal life because she and Cole were going to be blissfully happy and to tabloids that was really boring.

He thought she was living in a dream world, because the tabloids weren't known for letting go of a good thing. And Tulip had turned out to be a reader magnet. She and Cole together, being all smoochy, smoochy gave them heart palpitations. Levi was happy for his brother, he really was, but the media was not something he would ever embrace.

His thoughts hit a snag as his gaze landed on a beautiful brunette with a shapely figure and her startlingly blue eyes slammed into him. He felt as if he'd been burned by a blue flame. Their gazes collided, tangled, and then she turned and mixed into the crowd on the other side of the dance floor. He just stood there, stunned, feeling as though his world had just collided with a meteorite.

He moved from his position on the outskirts of the party into the throng as the music to the bride and groom's dance neared the end. He searched, feeling almost frantic to catch a glimpse of her before something happened and she disappeared out of his life forever. Several people called his name; he nodded but kept moving.

Beck McCoy from Stonewall, another happily married man of recent days, called his name and tipped his hat. They often used Beck's Learjet charter service to travel these days as commercial flights were harder and harder to deal with. Bret had flown in from his bull-riding event using McCoy Charters just so he could get to the wedding on time, and he'd fly out later tonight in order to be back for tomorrow's nationally televised event.

"You look like you're looking for a woman," Beck said, not holding him up.

"Yeah, about five foot eight, brunette, with amazing eyes. Did you see her pass by here?"

Beck's lip hitched upward. "Can't say that I did. But then, I had my eyes on that sweet little blue-eyed blonde." He nodded toward his wife, who danced on the edge of the floor with a small girl. They were laughing and happy, and he could see why Beck didn't see anyone in the room but his wife.

Just then, he saw her. A camera lifted in her hand as she snapped several shots of Cole dipping Tulip to the end of the wedding song and then planting a long, deeply involved kiss on his bride.

The blue-eyed beauty kept snapping photos—not like a normal partygoer would take a few; this woman was taking them consecutively, wanting the perfect shot. The money shot.

And then he knew, without doubt, that this was no guest. This was one of them, the photo jerks who crashed weddings of the wealthy, famous, or otherwise sought-after by the media for pictures to post. Photogs looking for their money shot to make a paycheck.

This wedding list had been meticulously cleaned to make certain no photo opportunist would get in.

But here she was, and he planned to take those photographs off her hands. Striding forward, he neared her just as she spotted him. Looking guilty as sin, she backed up, pocketed the small camera, and took off through the crowd.

And he was in hot pursuit. She was not getting off the property with that camera.

Dear Reader, I hope you enjoyed Cole and Tulip's story…which continues in the next book along with Levi's love story with the mysterious wedding crasher! And what about Jake and the other brothers? Don't miss a moment get Billionaire Cowboy's Wedding Crasher book 2 of the Billionaire Cowboys of True Love Texas series now.

As always, I appreciate you and thank you for coming on this story telling journey with me!

Happy reading!

Also from Hope Moore

Thank you for reading! Want to be the first to know about exclusive promotions, news, giveaways and new releases? Sign up for my newsletter here:

www.subscribepage.com/hopemooresignup

Reviews help other readers find new books. I always appreciate when my readers take time to leave and honest review. It is so helpful to me!

I love hearing from my readers. Please feel free to contact me at authorhopemoore@gmail.com

About the Author

Hope Moore is the pen name of an award-winning author who lives deep in the heart of Texas surrounded by Christian cowboys who give her inspiration for all of her inspirational sweet romances. She loves writing clean & wholesome, swoon worthy romances for all of her fans to enjoy and share with everyone. Her heartwarming, feel good romances are full of humor and heart, and gorgeous cowboys and heroes to love. And the spunky women they fall in love with and live happily-ever-after.

When she isn't writing, she's trying very hard not to cook, since she could live on peanut butter sandwiches, shredded wheat, coffee...and cheesecake why should she cook? She loves writing though and creating new stories is her passion. Though she does love shoes, she's admitted she has an addiction and tries really hard to stay out of shoe stores. She, however, is not addicted to social media and chooses to write instead of surf FB - but she LOVES her readers so she's working on a free novella just for you and if you sign up for her newsletter she will send it to you as soon as its ready! You'll also receive snippets of her adventures, along with special deals, sneak peaks of soon-to-be released books and of course any sales she might be having.

She promises she will not spam you, she hates to be spammed also, so she wouldn't dare do that to people she's crazy about (that means YOU). You can unsubscribe at any time.

Sign up for my newsletter:
www.subscribepage.com/hopemooresignup

I can't wait to hear from you.

Hope Moore~
Always hoping for more love, laughter and reading for you every day of your life!